'The short-story writer is sometim[...] novelist . . . Erica Wagner's debu[...] notion: she writes with such extant, feorile vitality as occasionally to make the short story look like some new-fangled idea of hers . . . Wagner has a talent for suspense that is so deft it conceals its craft.' Maggie O'Farrell, *New Statesman & Society*

'*Gravity* is that rare treasure, a collection of stories that reminds us of what fiction can, and should, do: render the strange familiar and the familiar strange; make the world new.' Claire Messud

'The quality of Erica Wagner's prose in her first collection of short stories is immediately obvious . . . it is the way she is seemingly able to create suspense out of thin air that is astonishing . . . Wagner's great gift proves to be her ability to transform bleak situations through the careful geometry of her prose, which resonates with the redeeming mysteries of life.' Frank Egerton, *Literary Review*

'Wagner writes exceptionally well and with much inventiveness and originality . . . Consistently understated, this is a prose which achieves its impact by stealth, with an economy of style which recalls Raymond Carver.' *Guardian*

'Grips with an intensity rarely found these days . . . There's a prodigious talent at work here.' *New Scientist*

'passionate, considered and imaginatively different' Julie Myerson, *Mail on Sunday*

'A dazzlingly versatile short-story collection that shows Wagner to be one of the most talented young writers around . . . Short-story writing has long been neglected by the publishing industry. Wagner should change that.' *Cosmopolitan* 'an enviable achievement' *Financial Times*

'One thinks of Poe – of the inexorable illogic of physical events. One thinks of Carver, because here so many still waters run deep . . . a voice with perfect pitch.' *Independent*

'Erica Wagner highlights the hidden strangeness in people's lives . . . The stories are beautifully poised and astonishingly assured.' *Observer*

'beautifully imagined and controlled' *Spectator*

'The language of these stories is polished and precise, their emotions intense. Savour them slowly.' *Options*

'Wagner performs a startling examination of our dislocated lives.' *Big Issue*

'Wagner's characters reach out awkwardly, separated from each other by emotional cling-film. The moment when the author peels this away is always worth waiting for.' *Daily Telegraph*

'Wagner fuels her collection with a restless, seeking energy, with a sense of destinations . . . [*Gravity*] is a harbinger of a new and welcome talent in the ascendant.' *Scotland on Sunday*

'These stories of pyramids, lions, haircuts and humanity are shaped by meticulous and evocative writing. Worth reading slowly.' *D-Tour*

Gravity

Erica Wagner was born in New York in 1967. Since 1986, she has lived in the UK, and she is now Literary Editor of *The Times*. Her short stories have appeared in magazines and anthologies, and have been broadcast on the radio. *Gravity* is her first book.

Gravity

stories

ERICA WAGNER

Granta Books
London

Granta Publications, 2/3 Hanover Yard, London N1 8BE
First published in Great Britain by Granta Books 1997
This edition publised by Granta Books 1998

'The Great Leonardo' first appeared in *Critical Quarterly*
(1992); 'Pyramid' in *The Catch* (Serpent's Tail, 1992);
'Mysteries of the Ancients' in *Backrubs* (Serpent's Tail, 1994);
'Stealing' in *Image* (1993/4). 'The Bends' and 'Please Don't'
have both been broadcast on BBC Radio 4.

Quotations in 'Gravity' taken from: *POWERS OF TEN: A
BOOK ABOUT THE RELATIVE SIZE OF THINGS IN
THE UNIVERSE* by Philip Morrison and Phylis Morrison ©
1992 by Scientific American Library. Used with permission of
W.H. Freeman and Company.

A CIP catalogue record for this book is
available from the British Library.

1 3 5 7 9 10 8 6 4 2

Typeset in Bembo by M Rules
Printed and bound in Great Britain by
Mackays of Chatham plc.

Contents

Gravity 1

Stealing 29

Please Don't 43

A Monkey 53

How Many There Are,

How Fast They Go,

The Direction They Go In 71

The Great Leonardo 85

Haircut 105

Jamie 117

A Simple Question 131

Pyramid 151

A Few Hours at Home 163

The Bends 169

Back Home 179

Mysteries of the Ancients 197

for my parents
for Francis
with love

Gravity

I.

Of all our senses it is vision that most informs the mind. We are versatile diurnal primates with a big visual cortex; we use sunlit color in constant examination of the bright world, though we can also watch by night. Our nocturnal primate cousins mostly remain high in the trees of the forest, patiently hunting insects in the darkness.

Imagine them, our primate cousins. Caught wide-eyed in the stroboscopic prison of the millisecond: clinging with strangely human fingers to the bearded branches which are, as the saying goes, as numerous as the stars. All night, every night, watching the darkness to live, and when the sun begins to rise over the green canopy of the highest trees, curling into crevices and sleeping a dreamless, animal sleep.

Now, imagine me. Waking up with my throat closed and my

eyes gummed shut, waking up because it's cold and the thin polyester sheet and old airline blanket have fallen off of me. I kick in my sleep, and I do not dream. Scraping at my eyelashes with my fingernails, I squint at my watch, which tells me it is ten o'clock, and time to get up. Twenty-two hundred hours. From my cot I can also see the big sidereal clock by the mirror housing of the telescope, which tells me the real time. Astronomers age faster than other people; in my forty years on this planet I have lived, by my count, forty years and forty sidereal days, a set of numbers which seems to me significant; although I am, as yet, unable to say why.

How different am I from my distant relative, the staring lemur? Not much, I think. With my complex eye made of steel and polished glass I watch the swarms of myriad suns as they rush away from me, catching their light with my mirror as my ancestor catches it with his wildly exaggerate retina. Each of us exists only for this. I, of course, have a computer with which to catch my particular species of insect and a stereo so that a little Mozart – *Eine Kleine Nachtmusik*, or is that too bad a joke? – may drift out through the thin mountain air towards those burning points of light.

Sunlit colour means little to me. At night one sees further, more clearly, past the haze of atmosphere and without the distraction of other waking voices. My night vision is very keen and I saw her coming from a long way away, the jeep winding slowly up the road that runs like a thin blue vein on the skin of the mountain. I could not see her face, but I am sure I saw her long hair, blowing back from her skull in the cold night wind.

2

II.

Ours is a modular world, built out of the myriad replications of the simplest structures, structures that we are only now beginning to understand. Within the nucleus is the proton; within the proton, the interacting quarks. Within quarks? The magnetized rings and tubes that are our great accelerators, the ultramicroscope probes of our time, have not given the final answer.

Absolute silence is a rare thing. Stand in your quiet country lane on a deep and moonless night and you will still hear the distressed cricket, the nightjar, or the thin webbed wings of a bat as it brushes past your face. A dog will bark, and startle you. Here, there are no dogs and no bats either, and if the night is without wind, I can listen to my own heart beat and hear the blood rushing through the veins in my ears. Sometimes I will lie down on the hard metal grate of the floor and listen to myself. I know that however still I am, it is only illusory: not only does my blood rush and my chest rise and fall with my breathing, but the atoms that make up the cells of my body do their frantic dance within me, without my will or – were I more ignorant than I am – my knowledge.

Take the carbon atom, for instance. Common to us all, animal, mineral, vegetable. And if you and I twine our fingers together in an embrace, what are we but the same stuff? Even without the intrusive gaze of the electron microscope we see that the world is made up of common parts, that we ourselves are made up of common parts. A baby is born: and of this infant we say, she has her mother's eyes, her father's ears. Our mistakes are common. The parents of the baby say, we will not do to her what our parents did to us, but they beat the child just the same.

The elemental world fits together according to certain rules. Models can be built, tables drawn up, predictions accurately made. The doubt only arises because we still wish to learn what lies within: within and within and within.

But Victoria, like me, was one who looked out: a girl who grew up staring at the vast Colorado sky and wondering what lay beyond the crystal sphere so easily obscured by sunlight or smudged by cloud. Her eyes were wide-open, and bright sky-blue as if they had been stained by too much staring upwards, her lashes pale, bleached by the sun. That first night she parked the jeep around the back, and I heard her footsteps crunch around to the doorway. I could no longer see her: I had remained sitting in the partly opened dome of the observatory, letting the smoke of my cigarette float out into the night. She rang the bell. Some people are surprised that this place has a doorbell much like any other place, but it does, and so I went to answer it.

Her thick hair looked silver with starlight, and it was wind-blown and tangled. She ran her fingers through it, her face a little severe, or worried. Her breathing was rapid and somewhat strained; it takes a while to get used to the air up here. At first it can feel like someone has played a terrible trick, replaced the oxygen with water or helium and has asked you to breathe. You never get used to sleeping in it: it was this air that stopped my dreams.

'You'll hyperventilate if you're not careful,' I said. 'Slow down.'

'I know.' She sighed a couple of times and put her outspread hand on her breastbone, pushing against herself. Then she held it out to me, her eyes just level with mine, for she was tall, as tall as I.

'Dr Victoria Greenwood,' she said at last. 'You're expecting me, I think?'

There was hesitancy in her voice, though there was no need for it. I took her hand in mine, held it, shook it. Her grasp was strong and fearless, and it overrode her cautious question.

'Yes,' I said. 'I'm Davenport. Come in.'

Her hand had fit in mine like the piece of a puzzle left for years on a table. Sometimes you pass it by, stare, do nothing; sometimes you see a piece that fits and slide the ball and socket joint together. But there is a piece, that if found, lets you find all the others, lets you see the whole built out of these simple blocks. Only a handshake, but through her palm I could feel the basic matter of my world. This is what lies behind the electron, the proton, the quark. I did not mean to feel this. But I did.

III.

The world is not dual; that below and that above are one and the same. The difference is but distance and motion.

The nearest star to us is Alpha Centauri, the brightest star in the constellation the Centaur and one not so different in its mass and brightness from our own sun. It is a little more than four light-years away. Light travels at 186,000 miles every second and so, in the vacuum of space, five trillion, eight hundred and seventy-eight billion miles in one year. Therefore Alpha Centauri burns at a distance of twenty-five trillion, one hundred and and fifty-seven billion, eight hundred and forty million miles away. And the twinkle we see in the sky is a twinkle that left that star more than four years ago; we can never see its light *now*. Now, it may no longer exist. Does *now*, then, itself exist?

Again, I will ask you to imagine. Imagine the number 'twenty-five trillion'. Now imagine the possible non-existence of what we think of as the present moment. Can you imagine either of these things? I think not; not really. They are elusive, like dreams: it is as if one moment the thought is there and then – you are disturbed, something else intrudes – it is gone.

Therefore, although we say we live in a system which, however vast, is in the end all the same system, this does not prevent that which is only a little outside the system – separated from us but by the conceits we call distance and motion and time – from being unimaginable.

I do not mean to give the idea that I was alone in my mountain eyrie until Victoria arrived. Many people came. The observatory is a famous place. Whatever great revelations come out of the field of radio astronomy, the optical telescope will never die because of man's passionately visual nature. He wishes to see the stars, and he can never see a radio wave. Victoria was one of a steady stream of researchers, men and women, some who stayed for months, some who left the morning after they arrived, but who all looked through the great telescope and saw the pictures that it made; and felt the same wonder that Galileo felt when he first turned his lenses to the ships on the distant horizon. That wonder never changes. It is that wonder which kept me always on the mountain, the keeper of a magical beast which I loved as I had never loved anything before.

Victoria slipped easily into my nocturnal routine. We never spoke much. There was little need to. She had her work, and I had mine; and academics develop cautious, not easily broken habits of circumspection. But it was more than this, you know that already. It was as if the starlight was always in her hair, a thick silver fall down her back which moved like a beacon around the observatory, drawing my eyes to it when they should have been elsewhere. I watched her through the frame of the telescope, its white metal struts making a graceful cage for her to walk within as she watched and calculated and wrote. She would sit at one of the dull grey desks, bent over the page, that wondrous hair gripped in her right hand as she leaned on her forehead, scratching the paper with the stump of a pencil clutched tight in her left. Her arm curved backwards around her work so that it looked as it were painful for her to write, and the third finger of her left hand was slightly deformed from years of the pencil's pressure. Her hands were large, with blunt, square-cut nails, and on them she wore several wide silver rings made by Navaho Indians.

She looked up and saw me watching her. I blushed; and was half glad she was not too near.

'Coffee?' I said.

She looked at her watch. It was nearly dawn. 'Okay,' she said. She smiled at me. Victoria did not smile easily; it was not her natural expression. The few she bestowed on me I stored in a secret place. I had not known that place was in me.

I made the coffee and brought it to her, black and oily. She took the mug in both her hands and blew across the surface of the liquid, sending up curls of steam around her face.

'Thanks,' she said.

A lock of hair dropped down across her forehead and into her eyes, pale and delicate as cobweb. Without thinking I reached out and pushed it back, letting my fingers slip down the back of her head and land, for a second, on her shoulder. Then I pulled them back, like a man who has been burned.

We are separated by distance and motion. All of us. All of us swing like planets, or comets, or stars, each on our own cosmic path which is created by the four dimensions that lie between us. The desert of Arizona is cratered by the impact of an ancient asteroid and the dust of that collision darkened the light of the Sun for hundreds of years. Collision is to be avoided at all costs.

IV.

Individual atoms in a way have no history. They are identical . . . when atoms heal, their recovery is total. Even nuclear decay is ordered and modular; ageing uranium always turns into lead atoms of the right sort at the right rate. It is this stability even during change that marks the world of quantum motion, the world of modular identity.

I have a scar just under my lower lip. I got it when I was twelve: I fell out of a tree, flat on to my chest so the wind was knocked out of me, and I felt as if my face had split open. Dazed and choking, I wandered into the house, and my father held my shoulders as I leaned over the sink, helping me hold a cold and dripping cloth to my face while my mother called the doctor. I watched my blood swirl pinkly down the drain. I had to have three stitches.

Without this scar, and the accident that made it, would my life have been different? Would some crucial event not have occurred? On the surface it seems a minor incident, something of little matter except to make me, in my twelve-year-old guise, feel brave and foolish all at once, to let me taste my own blood. But we are woven of such stuff. We are made like quilts, over time and with many hands, drawn together into what we are and not knowing which stitch it is that makes us whole; which stitch, if removed, would unravel the entire fabric.

Without the scar on my lip – it is barely visible – would I have become an astronomer? Would Victoria?

I never asked her history. I did not need to. It was enough for me that she shared my code, the astronomer's all-encompassing tongue. Two people lean closely over the screen of the computer, and with their hands together they call up an image of the night sky as it was ten thousand years ago, as it will be ten thousand years hence. What language is there beyond this?

But we come at each other blind. We are polluted by our histories; attracted with the elegant inevitability of the electron, but made unpredictable by our scars and dreams. We cannot predict the rate of decay and we become unstable and unbalance the equation. It is only then that the questions are asked, the crucial questions that lead to words and blows. Or at least, that is how it seemed to me. It is a reversal of the process: it is being able to watch the smoothly locked element of lead splinter out, radiating heat and damage.

V.

*The limitation of the static image is not simply that it lacks the
flaw that marks our visual perception of motion . . . the deeper
lack is of content. A single take belies the manifold event.*

Victoria comes into my room shortly after dawn. Turns the
handle on the door, pushes it forward; it is unlocked. I am
awake, lying on my back, and my eyes are still open. I can see
her quite clearly in the dim light. I can see her open her mouth
as if she would speak, and then change her mind and close it.
Her lips press together tightly. She is wearing a robe, like a
kimono, holding it shut at her chest. Then she lets go, and
flexes her shoulders back, and it drops to the floor.

Her mouth tastes of toothpaste and a little of coffee and
cigarettes, like the memory of a taste. I have pulled her down to
me, fast, shooting up out of my narrow bed like a snake strik-
ing and wanting to swallow her, as if this were the only way I
could get close enough to her. Now her mouth is the sea:
shining, sea-washed pebbles of teeth and her tongue with the
softness of anemone, reaching out and recoiling. We breathe
each other's air, and I have a sudden vision of another woman,
long ago, who looked at me and said, I want you inside me. I
want Victoria inside me. I would devour her.

Her body is different than I had imagined it. The clothing
she wears is loose, man's clothing that billows beneath the fine
bones of her face and hints at voluptuousness. There is none:
she is a pattern of lines and angles, delicate and fine as a bird. I

11

can count her ribs with the palm of my hand, and cup her soft breast easily. It is almost a childish body, it almost makes me ashamed. With her straight, visible bones and threads of taut muscle, she is a geometry of my desire.

The sun is rising. She is on top of me, so I can see the length of her, her arced back and high shoulders, her moving jaw. She is breathing, or speaking so I cannot hear. She looks at me, her eyes open so I think she must be seeing through me, and I ride against her, my thighs and hips sweating where she presses against me and I feel my orgasm building quickly in a hard knot at the pit of my stomach. I would wait but it will not, slamming me against the bed with the force of a wrecking ball. In its waves and wake Victoria is nothing, she is a vehicle, a vessel. I clutch at her waist and pull her down tight on to me, and I cry out. Her head bends forward, and she looks down; I think she is surprised and I am afraid she is disappointed.

In a moment I cannot move, chained to the bed in the aftermath of this explosion. Victoria says nothing, rubs my chest, and perhaps she smiles, but I cannot tell. I apologize, and then feel worse.

'It's all right,' she says. 'Next time.'

A single take belies the manifold event. A third imagining: that you had never seen or heard of the atom bomb. Now I show you a photograph of a tall, ringed cloud, rising, expanding in cumulus curls at its head. Without the distant wings of a Superfortress, without flash or fireball or devastation and blackened skin, what do you see except a cloud?

A hand rests against skin: a caress, or a slap.

A mouth bent to the soft hollow at the base of a throat: kissing, or biting.

And so I lie, so you see me lie, feeling myself wilt and shrink away from my star-crossed lover, breathless, head back, eyes closed. Victoria still, slumped over my unmoving form.

VI.

But look at the galaxies in collison, their long arms and counterarms telling a strange yet purely gravitational tale. Even the new compact objects, like the neutron stars, are understandable as the outcome of Newtonian pull, no less than the intricate rings of the planets are. The wild comets, never disciplined to the flat plane of the solar system, are occasionally imprisoned for indefinite sentences inside Jupiter's orbit. All these are signs of the versatility of gravitation. In effect, the whole world of the large is one drama of resistance to the inexorable, never saturated, never forgiving pull of gravity, from which its orbit, its high temperature, or its quantum motion may preserve a system, at least for a while.

Dropped from a tower, a ball will not stop falling of its own accord: it will rest when it hits the ground. A bullet will follow its curved trajectory, unless it is brought to a halt by its target.

I wonder, sometimes, if she had kept me simply in my terrible trance of attention, what would have happened. If perhaps she would just have moved out of my orbit, by her own effort or by some other sucking field unknown to me. By the battered, army-surplus jeep that rattled her up here in the first place. But it didn't work that way.

I tell myself, it was Victoria's will, Victoria's desire. Victoria came to me: that first night I could feel her skin burn and shudder beneath my hands, as much a victim as I. It had startled me: I remembered her cool eyes, remembered how I had thought I saw nothing in them, nothing that would indicate this. I was beginning to feel as if I carried a furnace in my head, that seared my eyelids when I blinked. I had seen nothing like that in Victoria's expression.

And so it remained. I called her a vehicle, a vessel. I thought that a failing in me. But I began to think that it was not, that it was an expression of what she was. She held me paralysed: the relief of my desperate, shaming desire brought me no relief from the startled distraction that ate away at my work. Because she did not grow warm. She remained a complete system, inviolate despite my violation. Her smiles were just as rare, her words just as few; and I could not redress the balance for my throat and mind were somehow stopped.

I told myself, over and over, that if I could simply get back to work everything would be all right. And I sat for hours in front of the cold coloured screen of my computer, seeing and not seeing, washed with misery when Victoria asked me if there was anything I needed.

I put my own research aside and did the work of others. There was always plenty of it. Requests from scientists in many fields for photographs of this or that cluster, charts of nebulae and maps of the moon. I grow vague. But it seems to me that I do not recall much of what I did then. And yet I could not run away: caught as I was in this inexorable gravitational pull. Never forgiving. The pull of the stars and the pull of the Victoria were one and the same, and I could leave neither. I was drawn down and cut adrift.

When she came to my room – that was always the way –

came and stood with her robe pulled tight about her straight frame, each time I would hope that I would find it, that I would reach the place I wanted to be. That was how I thought about it. It was as if it were inside her and I could never get deep enough, though I crawled across her smooth skin with searching deliberation. She was my work, she was my experiment. And yet she was the scientist and observer: her face serene and sensual, seeming to have little to do with me. One night, on my knees, gripping her at shoulder and hip and watching the curve of her spine in the half-light, I drove myself hard into her anus, so that she cried out. I did not feel any pleasure, not as such. It had hurt me as well; but before her eyes shut on me, I saw them wide and clear with shock, and my stomach warmed and I could almost see the thing I needed. That was the first time I wanted to hurt her.

VII.

> *Energy does not mean something close to sunshine, gasoline or*
> *jelly doughnuts; the technical meaning is clear, but altogether*
> *more abstract . . . Energy is a quantity that can be defined for*
> *any system; its value can be calculated, but not directly*
> *observed, by procedures that demand much detailed analysis of*
> *the system. Once the value is found, it holds without change*
> *during all the changes any system can undergo, thermal, chemi-*
> *cal, biological.*

What is love but energy? A complex abstract bound up within a complex body, a turbine to drive a machine. I was becoming a new engine, driven by an unchanging relentless force which seemed beyond my comprehension. How does the scientist analyze the system if he is inside it? How does he find its value?

So, one night, I left the observatory. With the key slipped in my back pocket and my hands in the pockets of my parka, I walked out on to the stony mountain, something I had not done in a long time. It is a barren place. There is not much that lives this high, and little comfort to be gained from the company of lichens. It is a rutted moonscape; and after my initial fascination with its strangeness, I did not feel much need to revisit it – I had come here for the sky, after all, and that I could see better from the warm bubble of my home.

There was a wind, blowing hard and seeming to come from all directions at once, slapping my back and chest and making my trousers flap against my legs; looking up I could see the atmosphere shift with the disturbance so that the stars flickered and twinkled: a bad night for seeing. I didn't know where I was going or what I was doing; when I think back I wonder if I wasn't testing myself, to see how far I could make myself go from Victoria.

I walked in circles around the white dome, aimless. There was no moon, and I stumbled in the darkness, and I was cold. The diameter of my circles increased slowly, and that is all I thought about, the observatory getting a little smaller in my vision, noticing this with an intensity that blew everything else out of my head.

Then I stepped on the tail of a bird. I heard the bones crunch under my shoe, a different sound than the sound of the coarse gravel: softer. I did not know at first exactly what it was, but there was a sense of flesh that made me step back quickly and peer down at the ground.

I don't know much about birds or animals. This bird was black, with a bright yellow beak, not too big, and its feathers, splayed in strange directions, were glossy against the dull rock. I guessed it was a blackbird, but I couldn't really say. The beak opened and shut, opened and shut, as if it were gasping. It did not belong this high, and I wondered how – by what error of navigation, for I do know that birds navigate by the stars – it had blundered up the mountain. Its wing was broken, fanned out along the ground, and now its tail too was damaged; looking closely I could see the splintered feathers.

I knew that I should kill it: twist its neck, like you do with chickens, put it out of its misery. I bent down and reached out towards it, and its feathers were as soft as fur under my cold fingers. The eyes were deep and black and without pity. They were bright beads that shone with the glint of basalt and seemed to see me as clearly as I saw them. 'I should kill it,' I said out loud, and my voice was soft against the wind, steam vanishing in the darkness. I picked up the bird, and it twisted its head to stare at me, the damaged wing flopping against my wrist. Then I put it down, stood up, and walked as quickly as I could back to the observatory.

I found Einstein's famous equation easily inside myself, as my love travelled far ahead of me, faster than I could have imagined, until it seemed to approach some critical speed and make my body, its unwilling carrier, heavier and heavier, more weighted with its freakish self. The equation $E = mc^2$ tells us that the energy contained in any particle of matter is equal to the mass of that body multiplied by the square of the velocity of light. It reveals the magnitude of the energy locked into the nuclei of atoms, explains how the sun and stars can burn without waning for billions of years, lets loose the secret of atomic energy. It shows that one kilogramme of coal, if converted entirely to energy, would yield twenty-five billion kilowatt hours of electricity.

It reveals the secret at the heart of the universe: that mass and energy are in fact equivalent. Matter is not inert, solid, of mass only; energy is not an invisible ether. The difference is only one of a temporary state.

The equation of passion is little different. It is as dangerous and flexible. An equation which, if found, reveals and destroys all, and it had taken me in its teeth as easily as the wind had taken the blackbird and flung it against the stones of the mountain.

VIII.

The learned Salviati asks early on in the first day of the dialogue in Galileo's graceful Discourses Concerning Two New Sciences (1638), 'For who does not see that a horse falling from a height of six or eight feet will break its bones, while a dog falling from the same height . . . will suffer no harm?'

If you could stand us together naked you would see who was the stronger. Victoria's body revealed itself to me slowly: at first, through the thick lens of my need, I failed to see it. She was, as I have said, far from the rounded sensuality that her clothes hinted at; she was reed thin, flexible (and I tested her joints until I heard them creak), and white as polished bone. Strange, for the country girl she claimed she was: but I hold no truths she spoke as sacred. And she was vain, I am sure, of her whiteness; she always smelled sweet and flowery, almost too much so, so that once, near the end, I recalled as I kissed her having heard that embalming fluid has a sweet and cloying scent. I never saw her bathe, but I can easily imagine her, standing damp in a towel, caressing her skin with her strong fingers, anointing herself with a delicate oil. Between her collarbone and neck lay a deep, rosy hollow.

I wonder what you think I am like, in this instant before I describe myself for you. What is your picture of The Astronomer? Have you seen the statue of Tycho Brahe, standing stiff as the iron it is in the wind, head craned back, the features stern and blank, around the neck an unexpected ruff, so that you find yourself thinking of Salome with the Baptist's head?

I am at least not cursed with Brahe's deformity: my even features are, I suppose, handsome. Victoria never told me so, but she would cradle my cheek in her hand and lay her cool mouth along the line of my jaw. I am something over six feet tall. At school, at college, I was good at hockey and football (much to their surprise, for they called me a 'grind' and 'grinds' aren't meant to play games) and I have kept the muscles I gained in my youth.

Looking at the two of us, side by side, you might find yourself wondering if my weight alone might not snap her pelvis like chalk beneath me. And then you might recall the fable of the oak and the reed.

It didn't take long, a few weeks, for me to break. I was broken through her. It was indeed as if I had swallowed her, so that she was myself, and one morning when she reached for her coffee I saw the blue bruise I had made on her wrist. I turned away from her, stared at the steel girders of the telescope and grabbed them, pressing my face against the metal. I waited for her to come to me, lift her arm and say, look at this, look what you have done to me. But she would not. And I did not know why.

It is easy to see that this was where the trouble lay, in the why. I never thought it was a question I would ever need to ask. More than once that day I turned to her to say, don't I hurt you? Or, are you afraid? Though I could see that she was not afraid, not afraid of anything: I like to think we were alike in that way. Solitary people will be brave like that: they never have occasion to meet their fears. I could see that if I dared ask she would shrug, or smile (a little), and keep her answers closed tight within the brittle cage of her chest.

IX.

The early philosophers tried to explain how wood could change to fire and ashes, how bread could nourish the hungry, how black iron might rust red. They had the idea that deep down below the size we perceive, matter was a web of small molecules — the atoms — whose incessant rearrangements account for all becomings . . . The atomic world is not just like the one in which our senses place us. To be sure, it is the same world, for we have found no other anywhere, but it is related to the world of familiar experience through the same curious blend of the marvellous and the homely that we find out there among the planets.

Love is not pure, as the poets have led us to believe. Love is flawed, unbalanced, contaminate. A love that was pure would be simple, unmarked by the anguish that mars so much of what is human. It is a straight tree that burns to black ash, wrought iron that rusts and crumbles, predetermined to disintegrate by its own intrinsic structure.

That is the only excuse I can make for myself. That this was, somehow, destined, by the nature of its very existence. And that I found myself in a world made strange. It was still my own world: I could recognize the objects in it, the rooms I lived in, the high white dome of the observatory, the night sky outside. I could stand where I had always stood, and trace the glimmering bowl of the Dipper with my eye, point to the North Star. Some day, not so long from our own time, this will change: some other star will guide us north. Nothing is as stable as we would like to think it. I had known that all along: and yet, when I began to fail to recognize myself, I became lost and frightened. I would have felt less fearful, I think, if I had awakened on Mars.

To me, she looked just the same. I had hardly ever seen her sleep – she never slept with me, she went back to her own quarters – and the face I found, lying two days ago at the base of the telescope, could have been a sleeping face, as serene and composed as the one she wore when she woke. One arm was flung back behind her head, the rings on her fingers catching the light, and the other curled round her waist, as if she were protecting herself. Her mouth and eyes were a little open; I could just see a thin line of shining white beneath her thick lashes. I bent down and put my hands on her shoulders; and looking at her closely I could see that her teeth were stained pink. Touching her throat, I could find no pulse.

We had been standing together at the top of the telescope when she slipped, walking along the topmost metal platform that hovers, seeming barely supported by its metal struts, near the crown of the dome. It is like a crow's nest on a high mast, and as precarious, with its perforated floor making it easy to catch a toe or a heel and fall. I did not push her, which is probably what you believe.

I did not push her. It seemed to me she fell slowly, turning her face to me and even crying out my name. In that instant I could see her wide eyes and hear in her cracking voice that she needed me; that she, in that moment before she fell, knew what need was like. And I also knew that she would never feel that need again, that I might save her and she might thank me, brush off her jeans, shake her hair, but that nothing would change. And that soon she would be gone, driving off down the mountain again and letting her pliant body be used by some other man, somewhere else, and that it would not make any difference to her. In that instant, our eyes met, and for the first time each of us saw the other's thoughts, and Victoria began to scream. I did not reach out my hand.

She smashed like an egg on the floor below. Looking more closely, I could see that the back of her head had stove in, and that the thick hair was beginning to be matted with blood. I had wanted to find out what was inside her, but even death had not released her essence; even lying so, flung out for me to study, I found nothing. Her still blue eyes would relinquish nothing, even were I to watch them melt into jelly.

I sat for a while by her shape, cross-legged, the way children sit. The blood puddled beneath her head so that it looked like a satin cushion, and her face grew paler, the lips a little blue. There are some who say that there are gravitational fields in space so strong that they might act as time machines; that could we survive their tremendous compression, we would emerge in ancient space, return to see a hot dust cloud spinning where we look for the blue eye of our home planet. We would find worlds strange and marvellous to us, suspended in the void of space: there would only be the void to recognize.

X.

As the size of a body increases, the self attraction arising from gravitational forces pulls internally on all portions of the object. Let the body become of great size, and no material has sufficient strength to withstand the effects of gravity. The object is self-compressed; it strains to become as compact as possible. Once it is massive enough, it must approximate a sphere . . . Astronomy is thus the regime of the sphere; no such thing as a teacup the size of Jupiter is possible in our world.

The red giant is a dying star. Cooling, expanding, reaching the end of its fuel supply, a thousand times the diameter of the sun. Nothing lasts forever. Stars, too, go out; like a hearth fire left to dwindle as the family sleeps. In its death throes, it will contract: cool completely, fold in on itself to become that concentration of matter we call a black hole, a teaspoon of whose matter weighs more than a ton. Dark and dense they hang in space, sucking in light, distorting radio waves, invisible except as disturbance.

I have called the university. They will call an ambulance, call the police, who will wonder why I have left Victoria lying for as long as I have. Her mouth and eyelids are quite blue now, the skin yellowy but even paler than before, and if I look beneath the collar of her shirt I can see the dark, bruise-like marks that show where her blood has puddled in her veins as it ceased to flow and was dragged down by gravity to the floor. I will say, I was in shock, I was all alone here; I do not think I will be lying. I will tell them, we were lovers.

It is always gravity in the end. Victoria brought down from her height like Galileo's spheres or Newton's apple; her blood pulled down towards the core of the earth; the doomed star. As for myself – I suppose it is just the same. Sitting here now, at the flickering screen of my computer, I can see myself collapsed inwards, contracted by a force invisible and all-pervasive. Gravity marks the bounds of the possible. I am sure they will ask if I want to leave here. I do not. From what better place can I observe my systaltic self, spinning alone on the earth in an expanding void?

Stealing

I started stealing at a very early age. I don't know why: it wasn't like I didn't always have everything I wanted. I stole quarters, first. I have always liked them; I still do. I like their bright silver coinness, and when I was young I think they seemed more like money to me than dollar bills, which would have been just as easy to get off my father's dresser. But quarters could be stacked in neat, copper-sided columns, short columns for single dollars, taller columns for larger amounts. One or two at a time I stole, nothing more, nothing I couldn't have asked for, but that wasn't the point. I had a special drawer where I kept them, pushed at the back behind a casual array of pencils and paperclips, behind all the erasers I'd bought and forgotten until they'd aged irreparably into hard shiny pink teeth. The stuff that kids have in drawers. With the quarters behind.

Every couple of months or so I spent my hoard on candy. There's the other thing: at that point, if I'd said to my parents,

'I feel like buying a lot of candy. I mean really a lot. I would like to buy a lot of candy and eat it all at once until I feel sick and can't eat any more,' I think they would have said, upon reflection, OK. It might have taken some persuading, sure, but even at the age of nine I had a good line in convincing arguments and my parents always liked to feel they were good about meeting my needs, as they say. But I'd never tell them: the secrecy was the point, just like the stealing. It was all part of a rhythm, a current of tension beneath my otherwise normal and happy life that kept me going. When I discovered stealing I discovered secrecy, and it was like discovering another sense, a second sight or hearing. It hummed in the background, always. Soft at school, soft at the zoo or the dinner table, loud as I hunched over my bed with a pile of Milk Duds in front of me, or sprawled out afterwards with a dark cocoa ring round my mouth and a belly full of molten lead.

But with anything, habituation dulls sensation. A couple of years later I stole a twenty from my mother's wallet and put it at the back of the drawer, held down at its corners with four gleaming quarters. This made me sweat, and I slunk around the house for days, waiting to be discovered. I couldn't quite imagine this happening, and yet I was sure it would: there was only the three of us, after all, and my parents were always sure enough that it was me who didn't clean the bathtub or put the scissors back where they belonged. But in vain I waited. Either she never noticed or she decided she'd dropped it or lost it or miscounted what she spent. I don't know: I never saw her standing over her yawning wallet, scratching her head and counting on her fingers. But it was a big jump, and I felt a lot guiltier about that than about the quarters. I even stopped taking those for a while, just keeping the four to hold down the bill in the darkness of my desk. And then in January, I finally spent it on a birthday present for my mother. Scented bath oil and talc. She was surprised. I said I'd been saving. I felt better. Soon I felt able, slowly, to lift some more tens and twenties, and didn't need to hoard them for gifts. They began to go like the quarters did, slowly, on chocolate and potato chips, on hours spent with Jane Austen and Madeleine L'Engle. When I look back, I wonder if you find things because you need them: a kind of serendipity. Like the way I found stealing. Because it was about that time that my mother sat me down and told me that my social life was about to blossom (she used the word blossom) and that there were things I should begin to consider. We were sitting at the kitchen table when she said this, me with a glass of orange juice, her with a cup of black coffee, into which she stared when I asked her what she meant. Finally she said, 'Grace.'

'Grace?' I asked. 'Who's Grace?' I really thought she meant a woman, some sort of social instructor. My school was all girls, and I could see that my mother, who had been brought up going to tea-parties and dances from the time she was four, might think I needed such a personage. I never even wore skirts much, except my school uniform. I began to imagine Grace, who had long, naturally curly hair and very red lips, and wore a stark white lab coat.

'No, no,' said my mother, taking a sip of her coffee and

smiling at me. 'Grace. Gracefulness. Poise.' She stopped. I stared. She looked nervous. We had never had an exchange like this before. She told me she had signed me up for dance classes, Saturday mornings at ten, somewhere on the East Side. I would love to learn to dance, she said.

That was when I learned that my mother thought I was fat. My mother, who as far as I knew had never thought anything bad about me before. And so I stole from her, and in my head, it evened things out. I guess I knew from the start that Grace and I would never see eye to eye: the stealing would keep Grace at bay. At first, the thing I did with the money was almost secondary, or anyway, I didn't think about it much. But now, my mother began to serve lean meats, crisp salads, mounds of snowy white cottage cheese, and my second secret became sabotage. I didn't have to pay with quarters now; I used dollar bills, and like a spy I went from one candystore to another lest I begin to be recognized ('Weren't you in here three days ago, young woman?'). I began to notice the bones in my mother's wrists, bones I could not see in my own. I continued to take money, and keep it in the back of the drawer, pulling it out from under the quarters when I needed it. It was a balance against all the shredded lettuce. The dark green bills still gave me a little dangerous thrill, but nothing like the first time, nothing like my memory of the pleasure that my gleaming silver towers had given me.

I hated the dance classes. Martha Graham. My mother bought me a maroon leotard that itched and dark-blue tights, out of the bottoms of which my feet protruded like stranded fish. Grace was not there to help me. The teacher, a nearly spherical Frenchwoman, taught us routines I could never remember and at the end of the class we had to dance across the floor alone, doing the steps. After a few classes I gave up and would just trot, noticing, in my leotard, the gentle bouncing of my thighs. Mademoiselle gave up on me. When I got home my mother would have made me lunch (tuna on melba toast, a poached chicken breast) and would have a treat for me, usually something from Éclair, a creamy bun or two fluorescent *petits fours*. I couldn't bear to tell her how much I hated the dance classes, I couldn't stand the thought of saying something like that outright. I couldn't cut them: that I knew she'd find out. And anyway, where would I go? Hang out in some dive on the East Side? Saturday mornings? And I could see why my mother, with her thin wrists and pretty smile, wanted me to have Grace in my life. She wanted me (both my parents said this a lot) to have the best; but I began to think that our ideas of what 'the best' was might be divergent.

It was the stealing, I think, that kept me from resentment. My secret life. The rest didn't matter. My waist disappeared entirely, and I began to have little rings at the base of my fingers where the flesh pushed out, overextended, beyond the bone. My mother was puzzled. She did not suspect. Once, over dinner, looking at me across a pile of steamed broccoli and a single grilled lambchop she asked me, 'You're not eating sweets after school, honey, are you?'

My father glanced at her, a look that seemed to me both

angry and bored, but he was out of this now. He'd never said much anyway.

'No,' I said. This was the first direct lie I ever told either of them. I blinked, and looked right into her eyes. They were wide open and attentive, inquiring, not accusing. She only wanted the best for me, remember? I was surprised at how easily that 'no' came out, as if it really were true. I suppose she imagined me strolling home from the bus, a Ring Ding in one hand and a greasy bag of Frito Lays in the other, munching and laughing with my friends, my back teeth clogged with chemical-sodden dough and salt. Well, it wasn't like that. It wasn't like that at all. That would be trivial. So the lie was not exactly that. I picked up a spray of broccoli and put it in my mouth.

'Do use a utensil,' my mother said, sighing. She was probably beginning to wish there *was* a Grace after all.

She said we would have my metabolism tested. She said 'we' like it was a decision we'd actually made together, and I didn't say anything. I had such a good relationship with my mother: everyone knew that. We were a model pair. How could I broach dissent? And by then, part of me was beginning to think she was right. Her thin wrists and flat stomach were getting to me. I would watch her in the bath and see how the skin shifted over the back of her ribs when she bent over to chase the soap, and I was not oblivious to the fact that I was by now a very different shape from my friends. They went up, I went out. As my mother had predicted, they began to talk about boys. I hung at the edges of these discussions and felt awkward. So we would have my metabolism tested.

'I'm sure it's that,' my mother said, as we walked to the hospital. I was taking a day off school to do this; there was a needle involved and I hated needles. Usually they made me faint. So my mother said we would indulge me; I could sit at home with my feet up afterwards. I thought what a nice person my mother was, and that I was lucky, and I held her hand as we walked down Tenth Avenue. It was a bright cold day, and the wind that blew off the river was dry and arctic.

'What happens if it is that?' I asked. I wondered if there would be more needles.

'I'm not sure,' she said thoughtfully. 'I suppose you'll have thyroid pills or something. Don't worry. We'll sort this out.'

I nodded. I could see the beginnings of one of my mother's missions in all this, this solving the problem of my body. Periodically my mother found something to which to attach herself, and then she would cling with unfailing zeal. All kinds of things, causes, events: I could remember a passionate fixation on the opera, spending all her free evenings at the Met around the corner, persuading her friends to go with her, buying a little tape machine on which she would play *Madame Butterfly* incessantly. My father made me dinner and shrugged because he knew what she was like. For a while it was the blind: she joined the Lighthouse (also around the corner) and spent every Sunday reading to blind people. Some blind people came to our house for dinner even, which I liked because I could stare at them and they wouldn't mind. I was seven at the time. My father shrugged through this too. The blind people were nice enough.

But my mother was a very convincing person. My father was the kind of man who wouldn't be convinced by anything unless he wanted to be, but most people aren't like that, myself included. And so I began to be convinced that the errand we were on was real, and that this blood test would come up with some numbers that would make my mother sigh with relief, and make my body melt away with the simple ingestion of some magic pill. Her metabolism was slow, that was all, she would say, smiling down at me, holding my hand, our bony wrists colliding.

I fainted when they put the needle in my arm, of course. I asked if I could lie down first, but the doctor, who looked like Marcus Welby with a handlebar moustache, told me not to be silly. He seemed annoyed that I was even there: I heard him talking to my mother in the waiting-room (while they left me sitting there, staring at this long needle and the little vials to hold my blood) and telling her that it's hardly ever a thyroid problem, and does your daughter get any exercise? She dances, my mother said.

But when I came to it was over, my mother was pulling the sweaty hairs off my forehead and telling me I was fine, and we'd get in a taxi now and go home. She helped me on with my coat and gloves, the way she used to when I was little. We didn't say anything in the cab; we stared ahead and I wondered if she'd tell me what the doctor had said to her, but she didn't. There were lines around her mouth and her jaw muscles twitched the way they always did when she was thinking; she would have to find some other solution to me if my blood was normal. It was funny to know she was sitting there, hoping I'd have something wrong with me.

The results took a week to come through. The doctor, Doctor Simmons, called my mother while I was at school to tell her that she didn't have to worry, everything was fine. That was just what he said, she repeated it when I got home. She stood in the kitchen, and I was at the table drinking a glass of bluish skim milk.

'Doctor Simmons called today. He said, not to worry, your metabolism is fine.' And she smiled, showing her teeth.

'That's good,' I said. I put down the glass of milk, which was half-finished, because I didn't want any more of it. Not only did I hate skim milk, but I felt a little sick, very suddenly, because of the lie in her smile. I don't know why people think children are stupid, think they don't understand what's going on in grown-ups' heads; it's not true. I knew much more then, I am sure, than I do now. I was like a wind harp then, one of those things they used to set into walls that the breezes would play, changing their notes at the slightest breath. My mother played on me like that, and I had to keep the harmony right, or I thought I did. And sometimes I did look down at myself in the bath and I would see what she saw, a white mountain of flesh that as it became stranger and stranger, more alien to her and her bird-like body, would become unlovable. Perhaps she would cease to believe that she had produced it, that it was her own.

And so I lied with her. Of course it was good that there was nothing wrong, but underneath that a panic: visible in the thready lines that tied up her mouth like the strings of a purse. Dance classes and skim milk. Blood tests. She was doing all she could. It wasn't her, it was me. Because I was eleven, that's what I wanted her to think. Because I was eleven, I couldn't begin to hate her. I could only keep stealing. I took a ten that night, smoothed it out beneath its quarter corner-weights, and went to sleep thinking of what I could spend it on the next day, of the route I would take home from school.

'Aren't you hungry?' Dad said. He had just finished his second helping of spaghetti, which we had once every couple of weeks because it was my favourite, even though it was not the best thing for the waistline, my mother said. She meant mine.

I had poked my (three ounces, dry weight) helping around on my plate. I'd had a couple of bites, not much.

'Not really,' I said. 'Don't know why.' I threaded another strand on to the tines of my fork and wound it around, slowly. It took four turns. Lifted it, put it in my mouth, chewed. Put my fork down.

My father mopped his plate with a piece of bread and looked at my mother. 'Is she eating enough?' he said. 'She never eats anymore.'

'Of course she does,' my mother said quickly. 'She's not wasting away, is she? So yes, she's eating enough.'

But I wasn't. Not at home at least, not where she could see

me. I had decided that I wouldn't fight her plan, that it would make her feel better if I just followed her regime, and that the easiest way to do this was simply to stop. All the food she served me, I wouldn't eat. I thought, I think I really thought, that's what she wanted. So every night for the past couple of weeks I had been pushing my healthy dinner around on my plate, bringing my packed lunches back with a couple of bites taken out of my sandwich, only a spoonful removed from my tub of cottage cheese, my apple still shiny and perfect. At first she commented, like my father did:

'Was anything wrong with your lunch?' and she looked concerned, her eyes wary.

'Nothing,' I said. 'I just wasn't hungry.'

And she liked those words. She wasn't hungry much, my mother, she ate like a bird, always did. It was a trait of her character that was prominent, because she made it so, telling people at dinner parties, in restaurants, whenever there was food around. She thought it was a good way to be: after all, if you ate like a bird you didn't get to look like me, did you? So she thought I was changing. Both of us, we picked at our food like sparrows, and my father sat in the middle eating for the family. It's funny, when I look back at this story I'm telling, I begin to think that my father's coming out of it pretty badly, like some oaf who just shrugs and gets on with his life, who doesn't care. But it isn't true. He cared. But what did he know? I never expected him to be anything other than what he was. He didn't think one way or the other about eating like a bird, whether it was a good or bad thing. But my mother liked it. Or at least, she stopped asking.

The money I stole I spent faster now, because it was what I had to feed myself with. Those months, I hardly ever ate anything sitting down, and hardly ever when I was indoors: I had slices of pizza walking down Lex, and a couple of hotdogs as I moved in the crowds on Fifth Avenue, a big twisted pretzel with bright yellow mustard as I crossed 79th Street. Sometimes I thought people stared, men especially, the way they do at fat people when they see them eat (the way I do now, if I think they won't see me), censorious. I carried a toothbrush: I would stop into the public library by our building before I got home from school and brush my teeth, so my mother couldn't possibly catch a whiff of cheese or sauerkraut. Of course she must have known I was eating, even then I couldn't quite fool myself enough to believe that my deception was perfect; like she said, I was the same size, I looked fine. Fine, that is: healthy. But not getting any smaller, certainly.

My mother was quiet for a while, about a month of this. I guess for a few weeks anyway she could really convince herself that I wasn't eating, and that I would swiftly begin to dwindle, to be svelte, to be the daughter she always wanted. Maybe she was puzzled, too, to find that she wasn't happy with what she had. The first ten years of my life she'd spent boasting to other people about me, so much so I was embarrassed to meet them ('Oh! But we've heard so much *about* you!'); and now she was ashamed. When she was my age, she and my grandmother used to have matching outfits, smart in stiff wool. I'd seen the photographs of this, newspaper clippings some of them, and tried to imagine myself with my mother, superimposed over the captions. Impossible. We were like Laurel and Hardy, a joke. I could see her smile getting tighter and tighter, could see how she dreaded going with me when I needed new clothes. We both dreaded it.

'That looks fine.'

'I don't know.'

'No really, it's sweet.'

'Oh, OK, I guess. What about this?'

'I think you should stick to darker colours, just now.'

She was holding on to *just now*. I remember her face very clearly from that time, how she looked when she said things like that to me. That pattern of lines around the mouth, the corners of her eyes. We were stealing from each other. It was all magnified, then; not just how she looked but everything, my long walks home from school like treks across a new terrain that it was my business to map, with every kerb and corner store marked on some synapse in my mind. Checking what was in her wallet. I don't remember much else, actually. I don't remember what I did with my friends, for instance. That kind of thing seemed like it was distracting from the real business of life, this battle I had with my mother.

In the end, of course, she dropped it, just like she dropped everything else, the opera, the blind. That's the one thing I can't quite remember though, how it happened: it seemed to just fade away. One day we were eating steamed broccoli and chicken with the skin peeled off, and then somehow there was meatloaf. I stopped going to dancing classes, and you'd think some discussion of this would hang in my mind, some crucial

41

argument over the table, but there's nothing. Maybe I wore her down, or maybe she just got bored. But I wonder about those friends she dragged to the Met. Are they still stuck, impassioned – did they catch it from her, and do they now find all their money spent on opera boxes and long silk dresses for opening nights, while she has moved on to some thing else, some other desire? She never even walks through Lincoln Center now. I wonder if she's like Typhoid Mary, a carrier, but always free of the infection herself. Some days I wonder if I'll tell her, tell her about the quarters and the bills and the lost afternoons that ate into my life and made my first husband say, Jeannie, I'd stay if you'd lose some weight – but I don't think I will.

Please Don't

It was a sheet of yellow lined paper, its left-hand edge frayed where it had been torn from a spiral binding. It settled peacefully over the hectic spill of books I had left disarrayed across my usual desk in the Round Reading Room, T13. I had gone to make some notes from the old catalogues, had swung my way all around to F and G and had returned with a new sheaf of request slips; preoccupied by calculating how long it would take the new books I wanted to arrive from Woolwich, I was almost in my seat before I saw it.

Please don't chew gum.

Now I *know* it's not allowed. But I'd just given up smoking. I'm not a popper, I'm not a snapper, the last time I blew any kind of bubble I was ten and the gum got caught in my hair. This gentle request – not a demand, but an entreaty: the pale, barely grey pencil strokes seeming abashed, the soft rake of the letters, the high P, the dipped G and the quiet flourish where the M tailed off – reminded me of my better self. A warm flush of shame crept up from my neck to my face. I crumpled up the note and aimed it at the bin. Bullseye.

I spat my gum into a tissue. Craning my neck around I tried to see if I could detect a smug smile of satisfaction wreathing the face of any nearby reader, but it was all bent heads and rushing pencils.

I didn't think any more about it.

It is easy to become distracted here. Doing someone else's research has its advantages. There's a certain lack of commitment which I'm forced to admit I find attractive. Always have. Or that's what I'd thought anyway, but I shouldn't get ahead of myself. There's also the chance of that serendipitous encounter, the sudden meeting with the book you never knew you were looking for – the leatherbound equivalent of the glance across a crowded room, so much more likely when you have strayed, wantonly, far beyond the confines of your own field. Hey, stranger, come on back to my desk. Even the staid books that circle the walls offer possibilities. Heraldry. Indexes to theses. *Hyamson's Dictionary of English Phrases*, 1922. Mine is a job well-suited to one promiscuous of mind.

This week it was Iceland. I suppose the guidebook-writers go to the places they describe so breathlessly, but I've learned too much these past few years ever to trust them again. It's left to the likes of me to tidy up the figures, the heights of the volcanoes, the acreage of the plains, the date of the Constitution's writing. With my pencil (*All inks are potentially harmful to books and you are requested to use pencils whenever possible*) and my index cards I am the authority behind the glamour, the tailor, the makeup artist, but there's no credit for me when the lights go up. Not that I've ever really cared. I like it here, where it is quiet and blue and I get left alone.

Or had, until now.

At lunchtime I decided to treat myself to a diversion. I don't quite trust the computer catalogues, they are concealed and miraculous, too good to be true – but they offer fine opportunities for drives down intriguing by-roads. From Iceland, guidebooks, it's not far to Icehouses and Icebergs; not subjects, you understand, that I've ever had a particular passion for, but it doesn't take much to stir my curiosity. That's all you have in here, curiosity. The library is an alembic, purifying emotion until there is nothing left but the satisfaction of the quest. I found: *The Icehouses of Britain, 1720-1831, Ice: A Culinary Adventure* and *Frozen Tomb: The Lost Secrets of Atlantis* by one Simon St John Frakes (promiscuous, I remind you). I returned to my seat half an hour later, relieved of three request slips and filled with a sense of anticipation.

Please don't sigh.

Yellow paper, frayed edge. Neat where I was not: aligned carefully with the lip of the desk, buckling where my sprawl of cards and HBs made hillocks on the leather plain. I'd seen it, this time, from the end of my row, xanthic, luminous. I stood above it, my hands on my hips like an outraged housewife confronted with an unexpected mess.

Please don't sigh.

My first thought, I have to admit, was: did I sigh? I couldn't remember sighing. A sigh: a long, deep and audible exhalation expressive of sadness, weariness, longing, etc. To my own knowledge I hadn't felt any of these things. I was working, moving forward, taking in weights and measures and distance and time, lost in someone else's frosty, volcanic world, fourteen degrees north of my own domed cocoon.

In any case, my breath was my business. Keeping quiet is one thing; regulations regarding the precise working of one's lungs are quite another. I swivelled around. Heads bent, still. Scritch of pencils, tap of keys for those electronically inclined. But then library loons aren't obvious. For the most part they are content to remain like the rest of us – indeed, they want to imagine they are like the rest of us – pursuing their important concerns with a singlemindedness that would put indiscriminate readers like me to shame. Simon St John Frakes, he would be one of them, his desk piled high (*You are requested whenever possible not to put in more than twelve applications for books in any one day*) with tomes on the truths of the old Gods and the wisdom of the Sphinx.

I picked up the note and walked smartly, straight across the library – usually I meander round, the circularity is part of the pleasure – to the information desk. The librarian, whose name I had never known despite the fact that I saw him nearly every day, smiled at me as I approached.

'Look at this,' I said, more loudly than I should have.

His brows flexed together in consternation. I didn't expect *you* to be a talker, they seemed to say. I pushed the note across to him. It had crumpled in my hand.

He lifted it carefully from the desk, and held it up before his eyes as if it were something he were privileged to see. He looked at it for rather longer than I thought was necessary; I shifted as I stood and heard my shoes creak in the silence. I had never noticed him before, not really – a man not that much older than myself, with narrow features and bright blue eyes. In his dark hair there were a few silver threads – or was that just how the light caught them? I had seen him sometimes, at the edge of my vision, explaining patiently to another stranger the arcane ways of the library, or joining a particular book with a particular reader, a kind of bibliothecarous marriage-broker. I had never asked him anything before. I knew my way around. I did not need him.

He looked up then, and there I was, staring. Two bright spots bloomed on his pale cheeks.

'Someone left it on my desk,' I said, 'while I was at the computers.'

'Who?' he asked, not unreasonably.

'I don't know.' Now I did sigh, and it seemed to me the corner of his mouth ticced up into half a smile. But when he spoke his voice was low and cautious.

'Well,' he said. 'There's not much I can do. Unless you know who it is.' I imagined he wished such things wouldn't disturb the rhythm of his days, his haven.

'All right,' I said, not much mollified. 'Thanks.' I turned to walk away.

'By the way,' he said, 'is that gum?'

I swallowed hard. 'Certainly not,' I said.

Now, this expedition didn't take me long. On the way back

to my seat I stopped very briefly at the catalogues to double-check a book number I might have miscopied, but I couldn't have been gone from my seat for more than ten minutes. So that when I saw the yellow sheet draped languidly across my books I looked down at the one in my hand; hadn't I taken the thing to the information desk? I had. Another was waiting for me.

I can't bear it when you're sad.

What? I didn't understand. And then I looked at the previous note, still bunched in my hand: *Please don't sigh. I can't bear it when you're sad.*

I sat down slowly. I rearranged my books and papers a little. I laid the two notes out alongside each other. Barely turning my head, I looked to the left: two seats away a blonde girl with a thick sweater and glasses, four old books with speckled pages, their spines turned away from me. I craned my neck: a spiral bound notebook – with white pages. To my right, three seats down: an older man, dark hair flecked with grey, two slim books about mathematics, a notebook computer, index cards, no pad at all.

I leaned down towards him. 'Excuse me,' I whispered. I had to say it twice, and then he jerked his head round, his eyes narrow, as if he had been woken from a sound sleep. 'Did you see anyone leave a note on my desk?' I picked up one of the yellow sheets and fluttered it in the air, keeping the writing turned away from him.

'Sorry,' he said hoarsely, 'wasn't paying attention.' And he turned back to the slumber of his endeavours.

For a moment I sat at my desk, my palms against its cool

surface, the room's colour and space washing over me like the sea. Everything had changed. Solitude was my business, my possession and profession, the long days linked to each other with a thin chain of silence. Most of my contact with the outside world was by fax or e-mail; spend long enough with yourself and you come to be your best and most comfortable companion, long dialogues held inside one head as fascinating as any that could be imagined between two. One is easy and comfortable; one doesn't argue; one is never late; one doesn't wake up in the night shouting and frighten two out of sleep. One curls into itself, hugs itself under the duvet, until it is convinced it is a whole unto itself.

It happens faster than you think.

I picked up a pencil. I put it down again. I straightened a set of index cards which itemized the components of Iceland's GNP (fish, mostly). And then I got up and walked to the North Library; I had left a book on reserve there, there was something I needed to check; something about the chemical composition of molten lava. I took some cards and my pencil and found a seat in the upstairs gallery. I was gone for nearly an hour and a half.

Returning to T13 I kept my eyes anywhere but where I was going. Expectation is created as swiftly as disappointment. A crack threaded its impudent way across the blue dome; the clock's minute hand jerked forward, and then back. A girl whose leather jacket had slumped to the floor drew her hand through her wild black hair. And then I turned left at my row and counted past the legs of the chairs until I reached 13, grabbing like a blind man at its back and dragging it away from the desk and only then, only just then, allowing my eyes to rest on where I knew my latest missive would be. There was a hole in my vision, just the shape of a yellow paper square with a tattered edge.

Nothing.

The breath left me as if someone had put a hand on my stomach and pushed. I pulled back the chair and looked under the desk: perhaps it had fallen, a passing coat-tail whisking it on to the carpet. I bent low and smelled dark brown wood, old books, old wool. I reached down to check the other side of the row and grabbed someone's shoe: cool leather jumped out of my grasp. 'Sorry,' I muttered, and straightened, and caught the crown of my head on the edge of the desk coming up.

Tears made my eyes hot before I could think what a ridiculous thing it is to cry over – hitting your head. But it works every time, or at least it does for me, and so I imagine there must be a reflex, some neural highway as straight as a Roman road between the reception of the whack and the activation of the tear ducts. I must look it up, I thought as I scrabbled around in the pocket of my jeans for a tissue, I must go back to the computers and type in *tears* or *cranium* or *impact*. I cradled my skull in my palm and sat up straight and willed myself to put everything except the weights and measures of Iceland out of my throbbing brain. The peace of the library was a thick velvet curtain I could draw across my mind, I could stand safely behind it. I was reminded of why I was here in the first place. I told myself that I was happy. I started to tidy my desk.

I had just made a space by my elbow when I heard the muffled rumble of the book cart, and three volumes were set down by my arm. *The Icehouses of Britain; Ice: A Culinary Adventure; Frozen Tomb.* I hardly noticed, I never had before, the hand that laid them gently down – except when it came to rest on my shoulder.

'Please don't cry.' The voice that belonged to the hand was low and warm, not a whisper, but not much more. 'That I really couldn't bear.' Which was when I turned to see the librarian – his eyes as blue as polar drift, the silver at his temple, the roses of colour still bright in his cheeks.

'Is it against the rules?' I asked.

'No,' he said. 'But like bottles of ink – it shouldn't be necessary anymore.'

A Monkey

There is a man, and there is a little boy. Both their ages are hard to determine: perhaps the man is twenty-five, but he could be thirty-five, too, in his cut-off jeans and sandals and faded cotton T-shirt. His clothes are old and he thinks nothing of them; when he arrived he might have thought they would allow him to blend in, but they have not accorded him that privilege. Even without his blond hair and big feet, his clothes make him something different. He wears small, steel-rimmed spectacles: his reddened, beak nose sweats beneath them. On his wrist is a cheap digital watch.

The boy might be two years old, and might be four; might be older or younger than that. His face is a sallow puzzle: triangular, the skin stretched just too tight across the flat plane of the bones, the pretty rose of his mouth made small with some emotion whose existence, but not whose nature, is also apparent in the stillness of his narrow, up-tilted eyes. His hair is raggedly cut, but recently washed: almost glossy and nearly black. He is wearing tiny plastic flip-flops and a shirt which appears to belong to the man: wrinkled cotton whose colour has long ago dimmed. The sleeves fall nearly to his wrists; the collar hangs off one thin shoulder and exposes a breastbone which looks like it might break through his skin, which looks as fragile as the skeleton of a bird.

The man and the boy are sitting across from each other. They watch each other, without knowing what they are look-ing for or what they might see. The man wonders if he looks like a monster, huge and pale and oafish. He smiles. But the bar is dark, even at eight o'clock on this brilliant northern morn-ing, and he is afraid his wan smile will disappear in the gloom. Already the heat has begun to glare back from the dusty pave-ments and seep into the wooden room. The whole bar is panelled with rough teak; the benches and tables sprout from the dark floor like mushrooms. The wood has been blackened with cigarette smoke, and several old and dusty tankards, in pewter and glass, hang above the bar proper. There are far more hooks than there are steins: the empty ones are curved and sharp. A carved wooden sign outside proclaims, in letters which are meant to be Gothic but which have been corrupted by the invasive curl of the native script: The Bier Stube.

He came here, the first day, because he couldn't help it. He had never been so foreign, and in the blazing afternoon he had seen what he thought was home, or something like it. Of course, he knew the moment the thought entered his head that it was wrong, that the Bier Stube was something worse than an imitation. But his solitude opened him to attachment: after that first day, he never went anywhere else.

A waiter comes over to them. There are three or four waiters in this place: mostly they sit at a table at the back, eating nuts and smoking cigarettes and shouting their conversation in exotic, excited birdcalls. They wear nylon shirts and thin trousers; they go barefoot. The man is forced to admit to himself that he cannot tell them apart.

'A beer,' he says, pointing to himself. He speaks in German, and he gestures broadly with his big hands. His voice is deep and very loud; he continues to hope that volume will effect some kind of translation. Generally he gets what he wants. The waiters hear his accent, and sometimes they laugh and call him Fritz – that is what he thinks they say. It is not his name.

'Eggs?' he says, pointing to the boy, who sits rigid in the face of this onslaught of alien yelling. 'Toast?' The man makes a heaping gesture, his hands over an imaginary plate. 'Breakfast?' He has never ordered food here before. The waiter looks at him blankly, but shows no inclination to leave; so the man says, 'Breakfast?' again, in English. He remembers a little of that, from school. The waiter nods, and goes away.

Last night he fed the boy noodles. He had bought them on the street, frightened by the thin, yellow face of his new and silent companion; bought them quickly and handed them down to the child, who took the bowl in hands made old by the streaks of blue veins running across them. The man had been hungry too, had been about to buy another bowl for

55

himself, but had found himself transfixed by the boy as he clawed down into the thick, oily noodles as if they might escape, shoving the steaming clumps into a mouth grown enormous with hunger. It had not occurred to him to wonder when the boy had last eaten, or what.

And then, the boy was sick. The noodles reappeared unchewed and undigested, blind white snakes making an explosive bid for freedom. It was over in a second, leaving the boy and the man startled and anxious. The noodle-seller's lined face erupted with laughter, like tree-bark split by an axe. She gave the man another bowl of noodles, and said something, not unkindly; that much he could tell. The boy reached for the bowl as if he would be happy to repeat the whole process again: but the man held it, bent down, and handed the boy the glutinous strips, one by one. He had not imagined this.

Now the waiter reappears, bearing a sweating bottle of Tiger beer and a plate of two eggs, fried and staring, and dry white toast. The bread here is strange: very light, tasting of nothing, like an imitation of bread. He lays these things down, and he lays down a pair of chopsticks, and a dented metal fork. The boy ignores the chopsticks, the fork, the waiter, the man: he takes an egg in his hand and will not let it slip out. The yolk, soft-cooked, breaks and puddles out between his fingers, which he licks with a sharp pink tongue. The man reaches out and touches his wrist, pulling the greasy fist a little away from the eager, sucking mouth. He is afraid the boy will be sick on the table. There are so many things to be afraid of: he had not known. The dark eyes (which are almost black, and seem to have no pupils) watch him. The white of the egg flops and drips. The tongue moves a little more slowly. The man drinks his beer in a single swallow. In drinking, he glances down to see the boy staring fascinated at his juggling throat.

He has been here a week. He took the train from Bangkok, overnight, sitting up wide awake and shivering in air that had been cooled to an arctic dryness. There were no blankets to be had, or if there were, they were being kept from him: in the endless hours between two and five that had been easy to believe. He had wished he had brought his cassette player. He sang to himself, pressing his face against the dark scratched glass and watching the night shuttle by outside. There were only isolated lights and the rocking of the train to tell him they were moving at all. He kept one hand curled around the bag strapped tight to his belly: the bag made him afraid to fall asleep. In it were his passport, the two airline tickets and the thick wad of American dollars his wife had handed him at the airport. I love you, she said. On the train he had tried to conjure her face from the darkness, her fine hair and pale skin. He had found it difficult.

He does not understand the money. When the waiter passes by again, he holds out a handful of paper and tarnished silver, and the waiter picks through it. The man cannot tell if he is seeking for the correct change or taking all the largest bills and coins, and he finds that he does not care. He remembers buying his train ticket, his fear that he was being cheated. It seems a very long time ago. The boy swings his legs and rubs at the surface of his empty plate with his finger. He has the composure of one who has already spent a very long time waiting.

The man stands up, and holds his hand out to the boy. 'Let's go,' he says. 'Come on.' The boy hops off the bench and reaches up for the outstretched hand: the man must bend slightly, from his great height, to take the fragile bundle of bones in his grasp. The man is grateful for the boy's easy allegiance; he believes it springs from the bowl of noodles. All last night the man had lain in an uneasy doze, waiting for the boy to cry, to reach out his arms for a vanished mother. But it had never happened. He had thrust his thumb into his mouth and fallen asleep, curled by the man's hip. He had wet the bed. The man had lifted him, holding him awkwardly in one arm while he stripped the sheets, balling them on the floor, and had placed the still-sleeping boy on the stained ticking of the mattress. The tang of urine, and his own metallic sweat, hung in his nostrils. He would wash in the morning. Each task faces him like an unexpected chasm in a path.

They will take the train back to Bangkok tonight. The man anticipates the familiarity of the train. He gropes for certainty in the hot light of the street. The avenue is broad, cutting across the centre of town, lined with shops and bars closed up tight like eyes screwed shut against the glare of day. They open slowly in the afternoon, spilling out on to the cracked pavement in a tumble of fruit and tyres and people; by night the air buzzes with fluorescence and is thick with the smell of scorched oil. The day yawns before him. A whole day! He wishes he could sleep all day, and make the boy sleep too. He wishes they could sleep until they reached Germany, until the boy was ten years old and he would tell him a story about a village, and a bar, and his father so frightened that the boy would break, or die. He feels dizzy, regretting his breakfast of beer: but below him the boy looks all right. He hangs by his hand against the man's thigh, and sways gently, like a palm leaf.

'Tomas,' the man says. The boy does not look up. He was told the boy's name, once: but he could not pronounce it. Tomas is the name of his wife's father. To the boy it must sound like just another foreign word, like eggs, like breakfast. 'Tomas,' he says again, and shakes the little hand in his own. Now, if he smiles, the boy will smile back: they pretend that is language.

And then he sees the red truck. It is a covered pick-up, like all the others: not very new, not very clean, with hard wooden benches installed in the back. It is idling across the street, the driver's thin brown legs hanging out the open door like drooping vines, the smoke from his cigarette curling out of the cab. The man realizes that they have been watched, and because he does not know why he imagines the driver will take the boy from him, that he is not a truck driver but a policeman, under-cover. The doubtful legality of his errand assails him. The driver of the red truck slams the door and makes a squealing U-turn across the road, jerking to halt a foot from the man: a cloud of dust, kicked up by the balding tyres, settles gently over the two figures. The boy blinks, and swats at his eyes.

The driver leans out the window. 'Taxi? Taxi?' he says. His face is wheedling and eager, and he grins down at the boy with a voracious enthusiasm.

The boy gazes at the truck in wonder: he reaches out towards it, like a benediction.

'Taxi?' the driver says again. 'Silk? Silver? Lacquer?'

The man understands that he is being asked about shopping. He has neither the money nor the inclination for bargain-hunting in Asia; he could not think about gifts now. But in the boy's fascination with the truck he sees the answer to their day. Distractedly, on the long flight from Berlin, he had tried to study a guidebook to this region; now, he recalls what he has read about the countryside, the surrounding hills.

'Church?' he says, in English. It is the only word he can remember, and it is not the right one. He tries again, louder, but the driver's grin grows broader and more vacant. So he waves in the air with his hands: it is almost the shape of a woman he makes, a woman with a pointed head. He points to the hills and up, and says, 'Church,' again. He puts his hands together, as if in prayer.

The driver watches this charade intently. He repeats the shape, with his own hands, a shadow of it, as if talking to him-self, and then shouts something in his own language, delightedly. His teeth are blackened stumps, like a burnt forest. He points to the hills, too, and nods vigorously to show he understands. He holds up eight fingers, and takes a coin out of his pocket to show what he means.

The man takes his money out of his pocket, and peers at the bills. He has enough. He doesn't care what it costs. The boy wants to ride in the truck, and the man wants him to ride in it. He is collecting the boy's desires – to eat, to sleep, to ride in a red truck up a mountain – into himself. He fears the one he will not satisfy, and wards it off with gifts. He hands the driver the money, and lifts the boy into the truck, pulling himself up after. He settles on the bench and carefully puts an arm about the boy's bony shoulder to steady him: the truck roars, and they thunder off, turning the day yellow with dust.

Very soon the man realizes that the ride will not be what he had imagined. He had remembered a drive through France with his parents, a small farm road with green fields to either side and the air at the horizon bright with the wind off the sea. His father, rolling down his window to thrust his finger out into the air and point at this house, or that tree, the places he had seen so long ago; and his mother, quiet, watching his father so that, as a boy he had wondered if she would cry. He remembered that was something he could not understand. But now it is his father's excited index finger, the high pitch of his voice that torments him, as he sits with this waxen child in their rattling, hurtling cage.

He cannot point at anything. The town disintegrates at its edge: seems to crumble like biscuit into expanses of half-cultivated fields littered with broken cement blocks. There are bullocks, sometimes with children behind them, sometimes not, whose curving horns and drooping throats look sculpted for ritual rather than ploughing. He cannot imagine cows like these in the fields he knew as a boy.

The child looks ahead, his mouth open. Surely the bullocks are not strange to him. But the landscape is blurred with speed: the cows, the isolated, stunted trees are dragged past as if sucked back into a vaccuum. The boy's head does not turn, does not follow objects as they pass: the man has the impression that the boy is watching a film.

For a while there are billboards: emphatic, acid-coloured, indecipherable, and behind them it appears a sort of suburb is being constructed. Shells of reinforced concrete rise up out of the broken earth, their sheared-off ledges and landings sprung with twisted iron wire like a fringe of thinning hair. Every building seems to be at the same stage of construction. It occurs to the man that perhaps these structures are being pulled down; it is impossible to tell. At the base of some, gangs of workmen squat around smoking fires. Traffic thickens and they slow: a workman peels off the scarf that shields his face from the dust. It is a woman's face. Most of the workers, he realizes, are women.

It is nearly an hour before the country begins to rise into foothills. The day has whitened with heat: a volcanic wind buffets through the truck, yanking their hair back from their faces and pushing it into their eyes. The man's glasses are filmed with a scrim of dust; he wipes them on his shirt, smearing them. The boy seems to have got used to the movement now: holding tight to the seat he twists himself around to see, and the man can see the tendons in his shoulders as he moves, the shoulders of a tiny man. The boy's contentment is too self-contained to provide any kind of reassurance.

The truck strains and protests: the driver drops into third, and then into second gear. What was a hill has become a mountain, one of the cloud-shadowed mirages he had seen, in the distance, from the town. They have come a long way. Now, as they climb, grinding along the narrow switchback road, the oppressive heat drops away, and a damp mist begins to insinuate itself into their open cabin. The landscape changes. The bleached yellow of the city gives way to a thick maze of pale smoky greens. Pine trees release their briny sap into the air; but their shapes are alien, with fine sprays of needles springing from a single head to bow in the damp air, their trunks twisted in elaborate obeisance. Beneath these skeletal umbrellas is a dense palm scrub, crowding against the side of the mountain. Leaves blow back to show veined undersides in silver and khaki, and the wind rushing through them makes a low moan. Below, huddling in the valleys between the blunted distant hills, are the bright green steps of rice fields, laid out in tidy layers. They are kidney-shaped to fit into the folds of the land, and they shimmer with grain and dark water. They are being worked by figures in wide straw hats and clothes in earth-coloured blues and reds. It looks like something the man has dreamed. The truck staggers upward.

The hair on his legs and arms has risen with the cold. The temperature has dropped sharply, and the mist gets heavier and wetter, begins to look like solid cloud. The boy holds the seat, as he did before, but now convulsive shivers run through his body like electricity. The man gathers the child into his lap, and the boy, after a moment's rigidity, puts his thin arms around his neck. The boy cranes his neck to see the hills stretching out below. They are warmer now. The man wonders if they should go back, but the boy's intent, serious face dissuades him.

'Tomas,' the man says. 'Tomas.' He does not know what else to say. He cannot describe what he sees. He has no idea where they are.

It is this that he is thinking when the truck stops as suddenly as if a tree had been felled before it. The boy and the man lurch forward together, and a gust of black, oil-tainted exhaust coughs into the cabin. Righting himself, the man sees the driver's face through the dirty rear window, gesturing to him: and then sees the six soldiers walking slowly towards the truck.

They are carrying small machine-guns, and they wear heavy coats lined with fur and belted at the waist, like the coats of Russian officers. They have warm hats with furred ear flaps. The man's first emotion is embarrassment: he is dressed for the beach. He shivers, and they see him shiver, and they smile, all at once, as if he has given a signal. Most of them are missing teeth.

One soldier has thin, shabby stripes of gold braid on the epaulets of his coat. This man slings his gun over his shoulder and climbs up into the cabin as if he had been expecting a lift. He looks around, kicks his boot against the floorboards, stretches and spits, then stares silently at the man and the boy. As they were approaching in their wide-skirted coats, the man had thought they were tall, were giant: now he sees they are all of them small, much smaller than he. The five soldiers surround the truck, clasp its sides, peer inside. Their guns hang at their waists.

There is a moment where nothing happens. The driver's face is pressed against the glass of the window; the boy sits still in the lap of the man. They are like an audience waiting for a play to begin. It is in this moment that the man realizes that no one in the world knows where he is. If he were never to return from this mountain, he would have vanished from the face of the earth. The officer speaks. He tilts his head back, slanting his eyes, so it seems to the man (towering above the officer, even as he sits) he is being looked down upon. The officer asks him a question.

'I'm sorry,' the man says. 'I don't understand.'

The officer laughs; his men echo his laugher. The sound ricochets around the interior of the truck. The boy is so still in the man's arms that it is like holding a doll. The officer asks a question again; whether it is the same question or another one the man cannot tell. It is peculiarly disconcerting to be spoken to in this way: as if he ought to understand, as if by not understanding he is only exhibiting an unwillingness to co-operate. He tries to sit as still as the boy; then he tries to look relaxed; he looks into the face of the officer with an expression he tries to build into more than bafflement and fear. He cannot look away from the officer's face. In it is contempt, or amusement, or both. He watches it like an oracle.

The soldiers' talk rattles in his ears, coarse and loud. He knows, at least, that they are mocking him: his thin clothes, his glasses – they point to their eyes – his stupidity. He can only wait. He wants to speak to the small stone statue he holds in his arms but is afraid that his own language will provoke them. They prowl around the truck like cats, banging its walls and tyres: the driver swivels his head and shouts. They ignore him.

The man does not appeal to the driver: he does not see the use.

One of the soldiers is taller than all the others. His coat is too short in the sleeves; his face is composed of angles of bones and his front teeth have gone, so that his breath whistles in his mouth. The skin of his face is pocked with scars, like a moonscape. He pokes his head through the rails of the cabin, and studies the boy, and the man, and then without speaking reaches into his pocket and produces a handful of lychees, which he holds out before the boy.

When the boy will not take them, the man holds out his hand. Half of the soldier's face twists in something like a smile, and he dumps the fruit into the man's hand. One lychee rolls to the floor and rests by the officer's boot. The officer's laugh is a harsh bark: and rising to leave the truck he brings his sole down hard on the fruit. The pink knobbled skin snaps, and the white flesh shoots wetly on to the dirty boards. The officer swings out the back, stumbles a little, his gunbelt clanging against the exhaust.

And then they are gone. They walk away, saying nothing, and the man can smell the acrid smoke of their cigarettes. He holds the lychees tight in his fist and stares at the spattered fruit on the floor; the driver revs the engine of the truck and they continue upward as if they had never stopped.

When the soldiers' hut disappears from view behind a curve, the man is released from his trance-like stillness. Clutching the boy roughly to him, he pounds on the glass that separates him from the driver. He shouts: and the sound is hollow and muted in the cloudy air. 'Turn around! Turn around!' He too shouts as if he will be understood. But he is not; the driver waves and smiles. For the first time, the boy begins to cry.

The fragile edifice the man has built dissolves in the boy's tears. They fall like a silent fountain, dripping steadily down the fragile, jaundiced face, and making two clear rivulets in the dust that coats the stalk of his neck. There is no noise. The boy curls into himself, drawing his knees up into the T-shirt, letting himself fall sideways as the truck jolts over a rut in the road.

The man kneels on the floor of the truck. The child's silent misery unnerves him utterly. It reminds him only of one thing: of his father, who in the last hours of his life seemed to abandon his cancerous body for some other realm inaccessible to his wife and son. He was not unconscious. He was simply not present. Once, during their vigil, they had seen tears stream down the old man's face, their cause as mysterious as the source of an ancient river. He is afraid this little boy's sorrow is some prelude to death. His fear is colder than the mountain air and he clutches at the boy, pulling him close to his chest, scattering the rest of the lychees like shot. At the same moment the truck judders to a halt and the man loses his balance, and closing his body around the boy's to protect him, lets himself go limp. He is a skier, and knows how to fall. The boy and the man tumble out of the back of the truck and land, to the man's astonishment, on a cold marble floor.

The boy sits up on his chest, unharmed; the man feels a lump rising on the back of his head. He reaches back to touch it and winces; the boy's still wet face watches him curiously. He has been startled out of his weeping. The driver opens his door;

shouts and waves, points upward. The man clambers to his feet, holding the boy against his hip.

Now they are in thick cloud. It surrounds them, and yet seems to float just out of their reach, hovering always just so far away. It has swallowed the forest beneath and the sky above: the temple floats upon it like a ship on a calm grey sea.

This place is not ancient. The edges of the red stone are sharp, recently carved, and the marble flags on which the man stands have not lost their polished sheen. The truck has stopped at the edge of a wide courtyard, a neat rectangle sliced from the side of the mountain. Around it are low grey walls, with friezes incised in red relief, as if there is another layer of stone beneath the slate-coloured granite. The friezes depict animals and people, tangled together as if embracing, or embattled; humans and beasts alike with rounded sensuous limbs that seem to have no bone beneath the flesh. Looking down over the walls the man assumes a vista of trees and paddy fields, but sees nothing but the undulating mist. Looking up, beyond a delicate flight of stone stairs with baleful dragons for banisters, the dome and spire of the temple withdraw behind a veil of cloud, reappearing like a mirage.

The driver hawks and spits out of the window of the cab. The boy's thumb is in his mouth; his other hand locked securely into the man's hair. As he climbs the stairs, the man counts them: there are thirty-six. It seems a kind of prayer to do so, the only kind he can make anymore. A god of numbers is the kind of god he might be able to understand. A god of the lottery: the god that finds him on an unknown mountain with a stranger's child in his arms. The boy is warm against his ribs. It is not so cold now, anyway: out of the hurtling truck there is almost no wind. When he counts the last step the man can taste a film of salt sweat on his upper lip. The door of the temple, a simple, open arch, yawns before him like the mouth of a cave.

In the shadowed gloom of the curved stone walls, the monkey's eyes are the only bright thing. Pale as the mist, it sits curled on the placid head of the Buddha, its long tail a furry chinstrap for the broad carved face. For a second its eyes catch the light like polished coins, piercing the saturated air with a metallic glitter. Its face, small and black, seems frowning, affronted at the disruption of its toilet, and it sits glowering, its fur spangled with beads of dew. In the temple there is a faint animal smell, or so the man imagines: suddenly the delicately quivering monkey seems the most living thing he has ever seen, radiating heat and light in this cold place. A place whose builders he cannot imagine: the dark gleaming surfaces of the temple, the face of the Buddha, seem as old as the mountain itself. He will never know why they came here, or what, precisely, they saw: he will never know what questions he ought to have asked. He presses his cheek against the boy's, and feels his own tears.

The monkey's eyes shine like stars. It crouches, clutching the ears of the statue in its neat black fingers, its tail coiled like a question mark behind. When it leaps, skittering across the icy floor and disappearing out into the forest below, it is as if it had never been.

How Many There Are,
How Fast They Go,
The Direction They Go In

Jackson's mother comes to the house and pulls down all the shades. It's the middle of a summer's day, with that heat out here that's like a weight, like pressure, and the sun so bright the sky goes white and the horizon shivers and blurs. A streak of sunlight slips in under the edge of the kitchen blind and lies indolently across the smudgy linoleum. Shirley stands in front of the window and blocks it.

'I'd rather have them up,' I say. Shirley makes weak, Iowa coffee and I'm clutching a mug of it, putting my face over the steam and drawing out beads of sweat from my skin. The air-conditioners broke last week. Jackson was going to fix them today. He said the vents were blocked with cat hair.

'Well, you can't,' Shirley says. 'It's not respectful. It's what you have to do.' She gives another tug at the blind behind her, her mouth pursed with correctness. The last time I saw her was more than six years ago, at our wedding, and she fussed with the hem of my dress like she fusses with the blind, and called me a motherless girl, and wore just the same face. Shirley looks soft but she's not. She's a big lady. She sheathes her bulk in pastel chiffons to keep the prickly heat at bay: she carries talc in her handbag. Her hair is a golden shade of Happy-To-Be-Me, and grieving does not stop her heating her rollers. Her eyes are the blue tips of steel rods behind her rhinestone glasses. She is a wonder to me. I wish she would go away.

I really want the blinds up. In the awkward silence I stare at the drooping pull. I see myself running wildly through the house, the shades snapping up behind me, whirling on their rollers, and Shirley lumbering after me, giant avenging angel of decorum. Shirley sees me smile and looks affronted.

'Are the children at school?'

'Yes.'

Through the ether I sense that sending the children to school is not What You Have To Do.

'It seemed the best thing,' I feel compelled to explain. 'It's bad enough as it is. They should be with their friends. They'd only sit around here all day – and do what?'

'Keep you company,' Shirley says, dauntless. 'Comfort you. They're all you have left.'

'Oh, Shirley,' I say. 'But I've got you.'

I met Jackson at a rodeo. We all used to go to rodeos at the weekends. We had gleaming white cowboy boots with steelcap toes, we had soft white felt stetsons with peacock feathers in the bands, we had suede jackets with long beaded fringes that swayed when we walked. I'm from New York. My first week-end at college in Austin my roommates took me and my Amex hostage and dragged us around the town. I thought the magnetic stripe on the card would wear away. My father was furious until he got the Polaroid I sent him. Who isn't a sucker for a cowgirl?

Jackson sat in the box next to us. Nita knew his friend, whose name I forget, and they bought us beers, and Jackson spilled his all over my boots. He dropped down on his knees in the sawdust and cigarette butts and mopped my feet with Kleenex. He had black hair and blue eyes and a broken front tooth.

'I love you,' he said.

Whenever you think Jackson's kidding, he isn't.

Jackson died like a lot of people do. Driving home late; arriving at the intersection just in time to appease the god who thought up Chaos Theory. A few seconds either way and we'd have sat at the kitchen table, drinking cocoa and holding hands and talking about a close shave. There's a lot of them round here. But instead of Jackson there was a policeman, and instead of cocoa we went to the morgue. That's how it was.

'Dad?'

I stood in the clean white corridor of the hospital and my voice echoed around the walls. There was no one much around. Nurses squeaked by in expensive sneakers, cast glances, walked on. My policeman sat around the corner with his hands in his lap, a sentry.

'Dad?'

'Honey?' My father was used to waking up quickly. My mother died when I was six. It was only us.

'Hi, Dad.'

'Where are you, hon? Are you OK?' I could hear him scrabbling for his glasses, all the way in New York City, in his dark bedroom snug as a ship's cabin.

'No. I'm home. I'm in Austin, I mean. At the hospital. Dad – Jackson's dead.' Deciding against the passive, was killed. It seemed a step away from the truth.

'Oh, honey. What happened?'

I told him. My voice was shaking but I didn't cry. I held on to my father at the other end of the line and I thought, we are old hands at this. My Dad knew for six months what was happening to my mother, they both knew, and all I knew was I was happier than I had ever been. There were picnics and stories and days off school and then she was gone and my Dad sat me on his shoulders in the brilliantly sunny cemetery, the other mourners, my cousins and aunts and uncles, glaring balefully in the inappropriate light.

'The car. Some drunk. You know.'

'I'm coming.'

'No, Dad. I've called Jackson's mother. She has to come. I can't – ' something hung in the air and then we both laughed. He met Shirley at the wedding. When I laughed the policeman poked his head around the corner and stared. Should I wave? I didn't.

'Wait a couple days. I'll call you tomorrow, Dad. Go back to sleep. I'll be OK. You know I will.'

Some things you say for other people. My Dad said a lot of them for me, once upon a time. He patched up a hole in me I never really knew I had. A little clumsily sometimes, but it held, and then Jackson papered over the cracks. Now Jackson was gone I was afraid of the hole, because now I was old enough to know what it was. Too old for my Dad to do anything about it.

'I know you will. You always are. Sometimes I think that's your trouble. You're like your mother.'

'I can't be, Dad,' I said. 'She's perfect. Perfect is only for stiffs.' And we laughed again, because we were allowed, because we had been through the wars.

Shirley and I drove to the funeral home. Chris and Jamie were with Jan, next door. They would have plenty of time to learn what had happened. There was no point in rushing them.

Once I'd identified Jackson ('Yes; that's him.' You never think you'll say it, do you?) and signed some papers, they'd taken him there. The hospital recommended the place: it was called the Carlton, like a hotel. A low stone building, very old-fashioned and sedate, with a dark-green awning shadowing the street. There was a parking lot out back. Shirley nosed the rented Buick into a space and turned the key. She didn't get out of the car.

'You don't have to put on a brave face for me,' she said. She looked straight ahead, at the sun-bleached brick back wall of the home.

'I'm not,' I said. Shirley's face was streaky; her eyes were watery; the armoury of pancake was gone. She had been fine until this morning. Then sitting across from me at the formica table she had suddenly blurred out of focus: the painted lines on her face ran together like rivers on a map. I got up and stood by the window and wished I hadn't. I felt sorry for her the way you do for an animal in a trap. And then I hated myself for thinking that, which made it worse. She hadn't said anything to me until now.

'Did he ever tell you how early I made him go to bed?' she asked. She kept looking at the wall.

'No,' I said. He never told me much about anything like that. Only that he wanted to leave.

'Well, I made him go to bed very early. Me and Wayne, we both thought it was the right thing. Keep him out of trouble. Six o'clock, mostly.'

'Until he was how old?'

'Sixteen.' She giggled. It escaped like flatulence. She put her hands in front of her mouth but I caught it from her, and I went too.

'Sixteen?'

'Honest to God. You know he stopped complaining, that was the thing. He used to sit up there and read. Just for hours. Anything he could lay his hands on. We had a mobile library used to come every week or so. For a while it was the movies:

he read everything about every movie he never saw, could tell you who was in 'em, when they made 'em, who put the lights on 'em. And he'd never seen one. We didn't even have a TV then. Wayne had some old encyclopædia he'd got for nothing one time, Jackson read that too, and then he'd sit having his dinner and talking and you'd swear he knew everything there ever was to know.'

The smile drifted off her face and she held the car keys tight.

'Just goes to show. No matter how much you know, you never know when it's coming.'

'Let's go inside,' I said.

The building was bigger than it looked. Inside it was expensive and sedate; a concierge, if that's what he was called, greeted us sombrely and we signed a register bound in blood-coloured leather. Mrs Shirley Dunn. Lucy Roberts Dunn. The concierge walked ahead of us, through several long, dark-carpeted corridors, turning corners, passing heavy oak doors, before we climbed a short flight of stairs and stopped in front of a door like all the others. How did he remember which was which? What would happen if it wasn't Jackson inside? Panic fluttered into my throat like a bird.

'This is a Chapel of Rest,' the concierge said. He had a low soothing voice, of which I am sure he was proud. 'Mr Dunn is in here. I think you'll find he's looking very peaceful.' The young man smiled at me gently. His words whistled past my head. I smiled back. 'I'll leave you in here for a few minutes with him; Mr Carlton will be along shortly.' He turned the handle and pushed open the door, then turned on his heel and left.

Shirley looked at me.

'You're all right?' she asked.

I was a ship she didn't know how to sail. She pulled on the wrong ropes; she let them run through her hands. Whatever happened in the car had vanished like it had never been.

'All right,' I said. We went in.

The room had no windows, and was lit by four small lamps with demure shades and bulbs the shape of candle-flames. It was light, but not too light. There were flowers in vases, lilies and carnations, and a heavy scent which may have been the flowers but probably was not. There were chairs with velvet seats. In the middle of the room was a long low table, and the coffin rested on that. It was very much larger than I thought it would be. It was lined with white fabric, and the top part of the lid was missing, removed from its hinges. Jackson was inside, or what used to be Jackson, wearing the blue suit the funeral home had come to collect that morning. It was his only suit.

'He looks like his father,' Shirley said. We were standing, one on either side of the coffin, like caryatids.

He didn't look like anything. He was wearing makeup. His mascara was clumping. I wanted to laugh. He was Not-Jackson.

We stood for a while, looking down at Not-Jackson, not speaking. Finally she looked up.

'My husband,' she said. 'It was like this. I should leave you with him. I should.' Her eyes were dry now. She came around to me and patted me gingerly on the shoulder, as if I were made out of something sticky, or fragile. 'I'll go back for a while. You should be with him. I'll be at the house. Don't worry about the children.'

Were we no longer related? Had we ever been? Imagining her younger, Jackson upstairs in his room: it was hard. She slipped out of the room before I could find something to say, and I was alone with the table and the coffin and the body.

I pulled up one of the velvet chairs, a little closer, not too close. And then this is what happened: I fell asleep.

We had driven out into the desert. It was the end of the semester; I was about to graduate, Jackson was about to finish his PhD. He was a mathematician, the first one I'd ever liked, and had a job in the radio-astronomy lab. There was a bottle of Wild Turkey rolling around at my feet and we shouldn't have been driving – I know that now – but there was no one on the road. It was a straight road, straight out into nothing, into flat sand and cactus and distant hills like the black backs of animals against the indigo of the sky. Behind us the city receded, the colour of a sinking sun.

Jackson put the radio on; it crackled like a rocket and he turned it off, and the wind raced in the windows past our ears. We had a full tank and we drove for a long time, drinking from the bottle sometimes and not saying much. I loved driving with Jackson. I didn't much care where we went. I loved being in the closed space of the car with him where nothing could get to us, where it was only gas stations and motels and fat stacks of blueberry pancakes for breakfast. My father always sent me money for airfare home at breaks; sometimes he sent me Jackson's airfare too. He liked Jackson. We always showed up three days later than we should have, dusty from the road, needing a shower and an oil-change.

It was nearly two in the morning when he finally pulled over, the car jolting across the blurred line that separated the road from the sea of dirty scrub around us. Jackson turned the key and the engine coughed and died; the noise of the wind was left, clattering along the sides of the car and rushing out to the horizon, which was visible only in so far as it was the place the stars began. It was a moonless night, a sparkling gift of a night, looped with the soft ribbon of the Milky Way.

Jackson put his arm around my shoulder and pulled me close to him. The gearshift poked into my thigh. He kissed me, and tasted of whiskey. It was too dark to see his eyes.

'Let's walk,' I said.

We left the car doors open. We leaned against each other like we were walking in a gale, but outside the rattling car the wind was more a breeze; it blew on my face and I felt almost sober. I pushed my nose into Jackson's shoulder. He never smelled of anything, not even of himself: only a little dry, like stone or sand.

We stopped. Jackson's crooked profile was etched in stars.

'What's that one?' I said. Pointing up. To the Big Dipper, I knew it was called that, but that was all I knew.

'I don't know,' Jackson said.

'You know,' I said.

'Which one?'

'At the end. The handle.'

'Arcturus,' he said. He took my hand and put his face next to mine, squinted and held my finger out, so we could both look along its line. 'Mizar. Vega. Someday Vega will be the Pole Star. We'll be very dead then. Polaris. Castor and Pollux, the twins.'

'That?' I moved our hands.

'Not a star,' he said. 'Satellite. Too bright.'

Holding my hand the names came off his tongue and I wondered what they meant to him. Betelgeuse and Rigel in Orion; Sirius, Procyon, Capella, Aldebaran. Fanciful names, names not like others – not like Dog, Water, Sky – as if the namers knew they might have other names, unpronouncable, made of something other than language. We lay down in the dust together and Jackson possessed the sky with his naming, and it seemed to me that he might be an oracle. What would I hear if he said my name? Would it be the future?

Jackson took my hand, which was sweaty, and put his head on my shoulder. He closed his eyes and was quiet.

'So many,' he said at last. 'So fast. Flying away from us faster than we can think. Everything rushing away from everything else.'

I pushed myself away from him because I had to be sick. It swelled in me suddenly, like a balloon. I leaned against the car and Jackson held my hair back from my face.

'I could be pregnant.' The minute I said it I knew it was true.

'It's OK,' Jackson said. 'No problem.'

We lay awhile in the car, the seats back as far as they would go. Couldn't see the sky. I slept for a while. When I woke up it was nearly dawn, and we were heading back to the city.

'Mrs Dunn?'

Big as a linebacker. Running to fat the way linebackers do when they're not catching the passes anymore. In the dim light his suit was almost black. I was leaning forward with my head against the bier.

'Mrs Dunn?'

He put his hand on my shoulder. It was warm, the size of a soup plate. I remembered where I was. It occurred to me that I should push myself away, jump back, stand up, but nothing much happened in my body when I gave it directions. I could smell the piney wood of the coffin, and the thick, sharp bite of varnish.

He squatted on his big haunches; he pulled up his dark suit at the knees, the way men always do. Who teaches them?

'Mrs Dunn. I'm Mr Carlton. I am so sorry to have to make your acquaintance in these sad circumstances.'

I stared at him. I couldn't find anything to say.

'I came in earlier, Mrs Dunn – '

'Lucy – '

'Lucy.' He smiled. It was a tasteful smile. No, it was a kind smile. I could see that when I looked properly. I was sorry he had to prove himself to me, but he did. His shirt was so pressed, his suit so appropriate, his teeth were so white, and Jackson was dead. That was why.

'I came in earlier. I saw you.'

In his head was the next word, asleep, I am sure, but he didn't say it. I was glad. Embarrassment was better than grief and it came on strong, my saviour. I didn't know how to act. I should know. My father should have told me. It should be in my blood, or something.

'I'm sorry,' I said.

'No,' he said. 'I just didn't want to disturb you.'

He'd left his hand on my shoulder, and I didn't mind, which surprised me. His breath smelled minty. He was handsome, like a football coach in the movies. I guessed he was closer to fifty than forty.

'I'm okay now,' I said. We were having this conversation and Jackson was in the room but not in it. 'Did you play football?'

He didn't even look surprised. 'Yes I did. For the University, a long time ago. I try to keep in shape.' He was rolling with the punches. Somewhere there was musak playing. We were in the celestial elevator.

'Jackson had a bad shoulder,' I said. 'He had to give it up.'

At which point I thought I would get up, I don't know why, but my knees weren't in it with me. I rose and buckled, and Not-Jackson's moon-placid face came tilting towards me, out of orbit.

'I've got you –' Old Spice and Dippety-doo, a real Texas man. His suit was rough but I was slippery as a pigskin and he had to hang on tight. One arm landed around my waist and a big paw held on to my wrist and he swung me away from the

bier and the coffin, towards the door where Shirley was suddenly standing, her mouth a pink-and-black O. She saw us,
dancing, almost laughing, spinning on the low-lit floor to a
faint canned tune in the distance.

Everything flying away from everything else, that's what
Jackson said. Only not always. Not just then. I'll remember
that.

The Great Leonardo

His heart was pounding now, like it always did just before he went out into the ring. He had imagined he would get used to it: that his palm, curled around the handle of the thin black whip, would cease to sweat, and that his chest would cease to feel constricted by the glittering silver leotard. He had always dusted his armpits with talc; shifting from foot to foot he felt the wet mineral slippery on his skin. He inhaled, flexed his arms, watched the muscle bunch like the back of a dolphin curving through water. Muscle he'd made, a penance, after peering, that first day, into the dim stinking gymnasium that looked a fit place for atonement. It was filled with twisted black and steel machinery, straps and iron weights, racks whereon he could stretch his thin white body into something new. At first, he did not know what to do. He watched the others, would not speak or ask, but saw them buckle their strong shapes into the instruments and pull, push, lift. No one met his eyes, and he was glad. It hurt, and he was glad. Thus was Adam made, he thought, built out of the dust. I will build myself. I will begin again.

It was a cold day, it was February, the first time she came into the church. He remembered her red nose, her red earlobes, and her fingers, when she pulled them out of her woollen gloves, delicate as spines of silver birch. She had opened her purse awkwardly, her cold hands clumsy, pulled out a coin and put it in the wall-box: it clattered loudly for there were so few beneath it. He smiled as he stood at the back of the church, a dustcloth in his hand, the sleeve of his cassock pushed up; but she did not. She did not see him. She walked quickly to a pew at the back and sat very still, her eyes on the altar, gripping the pew in front of her. She did not remove her coat. After a while she knelt, and leant her forehead on her hands. It was a broad forehead, square and very white, the hair pulled back off her face with a plain black band; an Alice-band, it was called, and she looked like Alice, with her grave face and straight back, her delicate hands and small feet. All these things he had noticed, as he stood by the altar, and found himself thinking it was as if he had never really seen anyone before, as if he had been blind.

But had he? He thought of some of his other parishioners and what they looked like: Mrs Arnold, with her thinning, dyed hair (always a little grey at the roots) and spectacles resting on her bosom, anchored to her body with a thin gold chain; Mark Andrews, his bright face leached of colour by his wife's recent death, towing his three small children dutifully, carefully, as if they might break or be snatched away as his wife had been.

No. He knew them well. And yet here, kneeling at the back of the church on a Wednesday afternoon, was a woman he had never before seen and yet in whom he suddenly saw the meaning of the words he had known all his life: *in our image, after our likeness.* He stared at her – her head was still bowed – and held the dustcloth very tight. Her shoulders rose and fell, a sigh or a sob, he did not know, and then her head came up and she saw him. He must still have been smiling, for now she smiled back, a tentative, momentary flutter.

He turned and walked quickly into the vestry.

The smell was just the same as when he was a little boy, only stronger. His father used to take him to the circus every year; there was a troupe that came each spring and set up their tent on the village green. It wasn't a very big circus, they didn't have elephants or lions, but it was a circus nonetheless, and he had loved it. There were white horses with sparkling bridles that trotted sedately round the ring while girls with taut, muscular thighs danced easily on their broad backs; there was a trapeze, and a Polish family who traversed the air above the ring, back and forth, up and down. His father bought him candyfloss and peanuts and they sat rapt, afraid for the Poles and their feats of daring, laughing at the clowns, admiring the horses and the pretty girls. And all afternoon there was a smell of sawdust and sweat, of the horseshit the clowns with their big brooms could never quite clear away, and of people packed too close together, their homes, their lives, all crammed in under the hot lights in the tent. His mother had not liked them to go; she thought it was wicked. She had told him that he ought to confess it on Sunday, confess going to the circus; but he never did. He knew it was not wicked; he did not want to give it away.

His mother was long dead. He could not have faced her now. And yet the circus scent in his nostrils called up her stern face, much easier to remember now she was so far gone. Perhaps she would not even have recognized him with his new, thick brown body, his hair slicked back and his blue eyes rimmed with kohl. This will make you look fierce, Lina had said, leaning over him, the soft black pencil pressed between her fingertips; open your eyes wide, look up. He had looked up high so that he could no longer see her, her white breasts blossoming from her tight sequinned bodice. He had blushed, and then thought, it does not matter anymore what I hold in my head, it is all mine. *And the man said, The woman whom thou gavest to be with me, she gave me of the tree, and I did eat.*

He began to wonder who she was and where she came from. She visited the church often, but never on Sundays; he had scanned the congregation for her serious face and had never seen it. Only in the afternoons, on weekdays, sometimes with a shopping basket over her arm which she would lay down by the door of the church as if it would be a profanity to bring it any farther in. He wondered if it would be; he did not think so. He had never thought of it that way, but was sure that she did.

He did not speak to her for many weeks. He knew that he ought to, for he knew that she was troubled. He was a good priest, a caring priest, and he recognized what he saw in her: her eyes too bright as she gazed at the altar, the fingers white-knuckled, clenched together with wrists pressed down hard on the wooden pew in front. He should go up to her as she stood by the collection-box (she always stood there for a few moments after she had pushed in her coins, indecisive, it seemed, as to whether to go or to stay), touch her arm, say, can I help you, my child?

But he could not. It was not that he was afraid, he could not call it fear; he just – could not. It pleased him when she came in: when he saw her, he would breathe a sigh of relief. Then he would place himself as far away from her as possible, in the opposite corner of the church, walking quietly, looking over his shoulder to catch glimpses of her bent head. It was clear that she did not wish to speak to him – did not wish to see the priest, he corrected himself. Not yet. He wondered if she would – surely she would – and then wondered what he would do.

He knew nothing about her. Only her little, thin hands, the small feet in plain shoes and slim ankles in thick stockings. He thought they were slim ankles; but he had not much experience of such things. He liked the sound of the two words together: slim ankles. The brown hair pulled back from her forehead, always the same, with the black band, no earrings, no jewellery that he could see. He wondered if she wore a cross at her throat. No makeup. Her face, below the wide, wise forehead, was not particularly pretty; the eyes were deep set and a little too close to the nose for what he knew was considered beauty; but her mouth was kind, relaxed, more relaxed than the rest of her, and a fine rose pink. Peering through the gloom of the church, he thought he could see the faint traces of lines around it; he guessed she was about his age.

He did not think of love, and he did not think of sin. He watched her face as he imagined he would watch the face of the Mother of God, should he ever see it. Her pale skin glowed in the light, in the faint flicker of the candles by which she knelt. He felt wonder.

Across from him, on the other side of the tent, they were rolling out the cages, one by one, linking them together to form a train of ferocity. It was quite dark in the wings, he could not see very clearly, but he could make out the shapes in the cages, moving, twisting in their small spaces, opening their jaws and pressing their fur against the bars. As they came closer to him, the note of the smell changed slightly, darkened with civet. He closed his eyes and inhaled. It was a splendid, dangerous smell, unlike anything else he knew. It was more texture than smell, so vividly did it conjure up the feel of thick fur – gold, orange, black, silver-spotted – of the slick blunt teeth and saw-toothed tongues rasping against his skin. He loved this: the hot scent in the moment before they met. He welcomed it, took it gratefully into his lungs. He knew they sensed his presence as much as he did theirs, and it made a vivid bridge between them, across the tent, across the ring, waiting for the moment when they would speak to each other and touch each other. At that moment, when the cages were opened, the ranks of seething, fidgety people became still, watching his glittering smoothness move so easily among the huge beasts. They would think, he has tamed them with his whip and his strength, but he knew that was not so. For in the ring, the love between them grew into a great searing sun that almost singed his flesh, hotter than the fiery hoops through which they leapt at his command. It was not so different from the old love, of incense and altar and velvet; it was only a new mystery. The sweat trickled down between his shoulders as he watched the clowns roll about the ring, run up and down in the dimness of the audience. It was almost time. The ringmaster was adjusting his brilliant coat, pulling on his tie, clearing his throat. In their cages, the cats waited. *My God hath sent his angel, and hath shut the lions' mouths, that they have not hurt me.*

In the end, of course, she came to confess. He was sitting quietly on the other side of the screen, reading in the half-light, wondering if anyone would come. People rarely did. Yet Mass was well attended; well, times change, he thought. Though it was not so long ago that he was young, and they all went to confession, his friends, his parents, their friends. He had enjoyed it, in a way. He had, in any case, never found it difficult. But then, he reflected, he had never really done anything wrong; and he could recall the priest chuckling as he gave him a few Hail Marys to say. Sin was never something of which he felt he had an adequate grasp. He wondered if that made him a lesser priest.

He was reading the Gospel of St John, because he liked the voice of Christ that he heard in it, human and mystical all at once. That was how he imagined him. A man you could sit down to dinner with, could laugh with and feel his arm solid around your shoulder, and yet who might at any moment say the most extraordinary thing, the thing that would change your life forever. It might be a little sly, it might be a little riddling, but if you thought hard enough you would come to understand.

If he read this gospel, he thought, he would understand. He read it carefully, moving his lips a little, practically whispering, with the image of the woman – whom he now called Mary in his mind – just in front of him, floating in the darkness. The deep eyes were like shadowy beams before him, boring into his flesh and causing him a nameless anguish. He could not find the sin, although he knew it was there. It must be lust, he thought. This is the sin of lust. He tried (he could not do it for very long) to imagine himself and the woman in a room, a room with a bed, where they were naked together, making love. He tried to imagine her voice crying to him, wanting him, and himself hot, burning, as he had been sometimes, pressing his skin against hers, her small breasts beneath his palms. He could go no farther than that. It was not that he felt horror or disgust; he just could not go on. It was not in him. So he thought, perhaps it is not lust: and then the vision of her seemed holy. He was afraid to discover that lust might wear a cloak of holiness. Michelangelo had painted the serpent with the torso of a beautiful woman. Such things were well known. *I said therefore unto you, that ye shall die in your sins: for if ye believe not that I am he, ye shall die in your sins. Then said they unto him, Who art thou? And Jesus saith unto them, Even the same that I said unto you from the beginning.*

The ringmaster strode into the ring, long steps in his high shining boots. He was a good man, the ringmaster, a man with faith. His name was Arthur Smith. He had had faith in the hollow-eyed, strong-bodied man who had come to him one day saying he wanted to be a lion-tamer. He had not laughed. He had looked down at his big red hands and nodded his head.

'Don't call it that anymore,' he had said.

'You don't?'

'No.' He looked solemn, appraising. 'Don't go down well. This cruelty business. All the fuss. You know. Working with the big cats, that's what we say now. Cat Men, that's what we call them.'

'Cat Men.'

He had told Arthur Smith that he had been a priest. Arthur Smith did not look surprised, but then he did not seem the kind of man who would be surprised at anything. He had looked him up and down and then taken hold of his arm and squeezed.

'D'you get muscles like that being a priest?'

'I haven't been a priest for a while,' he had said. He did not look into Arthur's eyes.

'Well. Muscular Christianity, I suppose. Why cats, then?'

He said nothing. He had not known. He had only wanted, been certain.

Arthur had been silent for a minute or so. 'Funnily enough, we're having a spot of trouble with our man. Don't say I said. Nerves, you know. Happens to the best of them. I like your face. Priest, you say? Go get yourself a broom, man, do a little sweeping. Get a little closer. Take care. See what you think.'

It seemed a long time ago, that afternoon. He had told no one else of his previous occupation, and believed that Arthur had kept the information to himself. He discovered that in circuses, people didn't ask. Many of them had grown up in the life and knew nothing else, but the others, drawn from the outside edges of society, appreciated discretion. Slowly, with cautious smiles, they had taken him in. He had, they said, a gift, and gifts they respected. The then Cat Man's nerves got worse, and he started drinking more and more. One morning, he was gone, and he left the glistening leather whip on the bed of the priest.

Now Arthur Smith moved swiftly into the tight circle of white light that swung out to meet him. He raised his hat; swung his arms; smiled, and bowed.

'Ladies and Gentlemen!' he called. 'Ladies and Gentlemen! The moment you have all been waiting for! What more can I say? He needs no introduction. Ladies and Gentlemen, I give you The Great Leonardo!'

A little hop off his toes and he was running into the light, his arms wide, his chest wide, his legs pushing him gracefully out into the centre ring, seeing the cages out of the corner of his eye roll out to meet him. The clowns and roustabouts pulled the barred train into a semi-circle behind him as he bowed deeply, before and behind, his head nearly brushing the sawdust on the ring floor, his face set still and stern. The crowd – from here they looked like dark bubbles on the surface of turbulent water – shouted and whistled and clapped, twirled their little torches to make small arcs of light.

The Great Leonardo let one arm drop slowly to his side and brought the other hand to his mouth, one finger on his lips, in an exaggerated gesture for silence. There was whispering, shuffling, giggles, and then quiet. He never spoke during the course of his act; the previous Cat Man had been hard of hearing, and had trained the animals with a series of gestures and claps. He had, however, spoken to his audience, told them of dangerous acts of daring, of the extraordinary skill of the animals, warned them of what was to come. The Great Leonardo did not open his mouth.

When he was a priest, his congregation always left the church whispering among themselves. What a beautiful voice he has, they said, so deep and musical. He had always known that this was so. He had liked to hear himself intoning the words of the service, in English, in Latin, letting his sermon (and how well he writes, they said, so simple and clear) roll off his tongue. Like wine in his mouth. He liked to begin his sermons with a reading from the Psalms, simply because he liked to feel the words resound in his head, floating over his palate, ringing in the small bones of his ears. *In thee, O Lord, do I put my trust: let me never be put to confusion. Deliver me in thy righteousness, and cause me to escape: incline thine ear unto me, and save me. Be thou my strong habitation, whereunto I may continually resort: thou hast given commandment to save me; for thou art my rock and my fortress.*

So now that he had escaped, he was silent. He abandoned his priestly vanity and became a thing of movement only, dwelling in his body only. It seemed fitting. His self was something entirely new, unrecognizable, and it was right, he thought, that he should find a new and different voice. And after all, to his real audience – to the great sleek cats –his beautiful solemn voice would mean nothing at all.

He clapped his hands twice. The roustabouts jumped to the front of the cages and turned keys in locks, six locks, six doors, six cages, six cats. The doors opened in a repeating curve, the roustabouts slipped out of the ring, and the cats glided out of their cages to sit in a circle around him. The audience began to applaud, and then, recalling his gesture, rustled quickly into silence.

There were two tigers, Sheba and Konrad. There were two leopards, called Silver and Gold because of their coats: Gold a leopard like any other but Silver seeming bleached and paled, his spots dark grey against his whitish coat. Orion was a black panther with knowing eyes like emeralds set in dark velvet.

Roland, tawny-bright with powerful shoulders and wide splayed paws, was a lion. Roland sat at the centre of the circle, looking out over Leonardo's shoulder. He was smaller than both Sheba and Konrad, who sat to either side of him, and yet it was he who commanded the most respect, who made the audience sigh and shudder. His movements were slow and dignified, and he seemed to act entirely of his own accord. His mane was thick, his fur gleaming under the lights. The Great Leonardo stood, a still centre in the breathing circle of blood and bone. Closing his eyes, he heard a tail twitching on sawdust, the rasping squeak of a yawn. He imagined the mouth that made it, peaceful and terrible all at once. Muscle quivered under skin. He raised his hands high, clapped once, and the circle opened and moved.

The door clicked open; he heard the sound of cloth moving against cloth, and then the creak of wood as she sat down on the seat. He knew, straightaway, that it was a woman who had entered the confessional: the anonymity of this office, he had very swiftly learned, was of a limited kind. Smells, speech rhythms, breathing patterns, all these were easily recognized. He did try not to notice such things, but he could not really help it. But he supposed it was the idea that was important: the small dark box, the little screen between the sinner and the priest creating a new identity for both.

He smelled plain soap, and heard a slight sigh. He felt the pressure of a body leaning against the wood of the confessional;

she would be leaning on his shoulder but for the planks between them. He was sure it was her. His hands grew cold and he clutched at his Bible, snapping it shut. She jumped. He swallowed, hoped that his voice would not break when he had to speak.

'Bless me, Father,' she said softly, and stopped. The voice was nondescript. No accent. Perhaps a little deep, deeper than he had expected. A little trembling in the 'a' of 'Father,' and then an anxious pause. He remained silent, waiting for her to finish the form. His mouth was dry, but he did not wish to clear his throat. He did not want to frighten her.

'Bless me, Father, for I have sinned,' she began again quickly, almost running the words together. 'It is a long time since my last confession . . .' The quiet voice trailed off, leaving the threat of tears in the air. He heard her breathing, imagining the harsh surface of her brown wool coat rising and falling too quickly.

What would it be that she had to confess, what sin? He realized, quite suddenly, that he did not want to know. Like lantern slides he saw projected in front of his eyes the images he held of her in his mind: the dark bent head, the narrow shoulders, the luminous eyes (in the darkness of the church he had never learned their colour) gazing at the altar as if it offered some healing, some answer.

Doubt and confusion struck him like a wave of the sea; he was tossed in the surf, his lungs filling with water, lost between the sand and the sky. He pressed his body against the wooden back of the confessional to stop himself shaking, and gripped his Bible until he began to lose feeling in the tips of his fingers. He did not wish to know her sin, he could not offer her anything, he would not say the right words. He would say to her, come out with me, talk with me, let me see the colour of your eyes, and is your name really Mary? He would ask to hear her speak: *My soul doth magnify the Lord, And my spirit hath rejoiced in God my Saviour. For he hath regarded the low estate of his handmaiden: for, behold, from henceforth all generations shall call me blessed.* He would watch the rosy mouth make the words of Mary over, make them for him. And that would be wrong.

He managed to speak, a little. 'I am sorry, my child,' he said, and clattered his way out of the confessional, the airless little box, sliding on the stones of the church to reach the vestry where he wrenched his shoulders trying to undo the back buttons on his cassock. He had it over his head, had torn his collar off, before he remembered that he had no other clothes in the church. He stood still in his underpants, shivering in the cold coloured light streaming through the pretty pointed windows that pierced the thick walls.

His predecessor had called himself Rufus, that was all. And no one had ever called him anything else outside of the ring: it suited him. Rufus had not been a particularly adventurous animal trainer; the act he had devised with his six cats was nothing very unusual: sitting up, rolling over, leaping over each other, jumping through hoops, jumping through flaming hoops. Only the leopards would do that, work with the flames.

Rufus had said that tigers had a terrible fear of fire – it had been something to get them to stay in the ring with it – and as for Roland, well, he probably would have done it but he'd never wanted to risk that beautiful mane. The priest, leaning against the cold steel bars of one of the cages, had nodded agreement. He had watched Rufus carefully, had charmed him, had been an acolyte. Had gone out and bought the bottles of gin that Rufus began to need, had not always asked to be reimbursed. They had both known what was happening. It was the only way.

There was little difference between the two men's acts, except for the silence. It is almost impossible to retrain big animals, animals that are not inclined to be trained in the first place: he had seen how difficult it had been for Rufus to make even the tiniest of changes. But The Great Leonardo was never bored or frustrated. He felt such absolute joy at being in the ring, alone, dancing with soft-furred death, leading them quietly through their paces. Feeling their love. There was a moment, near the end of the act, where The Great Leonardo would stand still, at the edge of the ring, as if he had forgotten what came next. He would turn to the audience, shrug. And the cats, arranged on their barrels, would watch him intently, willing him to come forward, or so it seemed. Finally, black Orion would leap from his perch and trot up to him, his thick tail held up like an ink stroke, and butt his head against the hand of The Great Leonardo, the corner of his soft mouth dragging against the skin so that the teeth grazed against his knuckles. He would sit, and look up with his chrysoprastic eyes, the pupils narrowing to slits as they faced the light. He purred. Like a cat by a hearth, he purred, rumbling, thunderous, deep in his throat, and the audience would whisper and ripple. And Ah yes, said the nod of The Great Leonardo. Ah yes; thank you, Orion: and he patted him on the head like a good child. They would trot back together to the centre of the ring, companions. And they were his companions, all of them.

He knew the act so well now that he barely needed to think about it. He could watch it going on before him, and feel the splendour of the animals around him, each a different size, a different texture, affecting him in a different way. It was, he admitted, a sensual pleasure, having them around him, and at first he had felt some guilt. And yet his heart was moved by so great a love for them that he felt it could not be evil. The love filled his body and his mind until everything else, all his past life, vanished utterly, and brought him peace, a peace he had never felt standing at the altar, giving out the bread and wine. Then, he had always been fearful, afraid of he knew not what – until she had come into the church and given a shape to his fear. With his strong arm he raised a silver hoop and watched them leap, Silver, Gold, Konrad, Sheba, Orion, Roland, moving the air around him, with the bending grace of trees in the wind and the terrific strength of ocean, sucking the fear from his soul. They were the seven stars in the sky. They were seven alike.

Now he stood at the side of the ring; now Orion came to fetch him, as always. He walked with long, loose-hipped strides, trying to feel that his pace matched Orion's, his fingers just brushing the dark fur. Orion leapt back on to his barrel, and Roland jumped down, coming forward to stand by The Great Leonardo.

It was the end of the act. He had never liked it very much, but the audience did, and so he kept it; it was easy enough. He leaned forward, and stretching out his arms brought his hands quickly together to his mouth, index fingers raised. Then slowly brought them out to the side again. His gaze was intense: absolute silence. The crowd, a dim sequence of shapes and circles, settled again in their seats. Their torches did not flicker. Their sweet smell hung in the air like a tapestry, woven in with the circus scent, a rich curtain around him. He let one arm drop so it rested on Roland's mane; grasped the fur with his fingers. He lowered himself down to his knees and faced the lion. They were eye to eye.

What did Roland think of his face? He always seemed to be gazing at it just as intently as his trainer stared at him. Roland had eyes the colour of antique gold, flecked with black and brown, and fur the colour of wheat shining in the sun. His broad nose was bent like a boxer's, and the fur there was thin, close over the bone, and scarred with a pattern of scratches like the lines of a map. Thick, wiry whiskers sprouted from beneath the nostrils, quivered in the air. The tongue rasped out, once, revealing the teeth which always protruded slightly – pearls resting on the black lip – to their full length. The yellowing canines were nearly an inch and a half long, and one of them, at the bottom, was gold. Roland was not a young lion. His breath was heavy and meaty, intoxicating. The Great Leonardo reached out, touched the lion under the chin, in the hollow between the bones where the flesh was soft and supple, and the lion opened his mouth wide.

For a second, The Great Leonardo peered into the yawning pinkness of the mouth, a mouth dappled with teeth and shining with saliva. He could see the opening of the throat. Then he shut his eyes, and turning his head a little to the side, slipped it easily into the lion's jaws.

The audience gasped. They always did. Though he could barely hear them; rushing breath surrounded him, and spilled into his ears and nose. He held himself very still, let the teeth scrape gently against his cheek. He reached up and stroked the tawny fur of the neck.

And then someone screamed. He could hear that easily enough: a hysterical, keening note that sounded as if it would tear the tent to pieces. Impossible to tell if it was a man or a woman. He felt the cats become uneasy, shift, grow confused, slope off the barrels and circle. Another scream. Someone else? He could not tell. His hand still on the neck of the lion he went to ease himself gently out, but found the jaws had stiffened. Beneath his palm the lion's pulse quickened, jarring against his own. Breathing. Pushing. A growl. And then he saw her again, her sweet, serious face, more vivid than ever, the eyes (he saw now) a deep sea-blue. Wet with tears, staring at the altar, and himself, trembling with his dustcloth, hovering at the back of the the church, the black cassock burning his body, the collar too tight around his throat, pulled tighter and tighter until he could not breathe, could only watch her staring and

103

weeping, the salt tears beginning to flow down her cheeks. *And at the ninth hour Jesus cried with a loud voice, saying, Eloi, Eloi, lama sabachthani? which is, being interpreted, My God, My God, why hast thou forsaken me?*

Haircut

6:30. I slap off the alarm and it falls off the table, cheeping again like a chick out of the nest.

'Jim –'

Linda puts her head under the pillow and her blonde hair fans out over her back. I grope on the floor and shut the thing up.

'Morning, honey.' It's amazing. I know I sound just the same. I've discovered something about myself, something I can do. The consolation prize. I haul myself out of bed and into the shower, pushing the water hotter and hotter until I can't take it anymore, and then one more notch, or two. The steam scours my lungs and fogs the mirror. I don't wipe it. I've discovered I like shaving this way, taking that little risk. Sometimes I close my eyes completely. It feels like skiing, those fast steep slopes when you don't know what's around the next bend. Mysterious. My own face. Three days ago it occurred to me that maybe I just can't stand to look at myself anymore, but I put that thought out of my head completely.

I leave the house like I always did. Camel jacket, nice tie. A present from Linda. Smart but casual, something out of a window at Saks. 7:15 and Lin's just awake, a steaming cup of coffee by her bed, brought to her by me. I said to her five years ago, Nothing's too good for you, sweetheart, and I meant it. I still do. Her face is soft and floury from sleep, without her makeup looking like anything might happen to it. It's a hard world out there. I lock the door behind me. I protect her. Not that she can't protect herself, believe me, she can, and she won't let you forget it. So I protect her, but I don't tell her. It's a secret between me and me.

I have a cup of coffee at Big Nick's round the corner. I buy the Times and read it, folded up into neat quarters, while I drink. I sit there for half an hour, maybe forty-five minutes. They don't mind. Stefano, he pours my second cup, he knows me. 'Mista Gol'man,' he says, and nods. I forget how he learned my name. I've been coming in here for years. I'm a good customer. Maybe I'll give him a tip at Christmas. Sometimes I think we're in a conspiracy, Stefano and me. But he doesn't know either. No one knows.

Eight o'clock and there's more than a buck shot. I have five. All ones, I keep them in my inside jacket pocket. A day's allowance.

It's getting cold now. I've got my tweed coat – Ralph

Lauren – over the camel jacket and a dark cashmere scarf wrapped tight around my throat. The air has that rasping winter bite, like someone slapping your cheeks. Wake up! it says. It also says: Get to work! but I don't listen to that one. I walk. I tell you, I'm a healthy guy these days. It's a good thing I never let myself buy a cheap pair of shoes. I've got a lot of mileage ahead of me. I tuck the paper under my arm and I set off at a good clip across the park. The naked trees arch over my head, like cathedral spires.

I'm a student of human nature. That's my new job. The old one, well – I guess I knew it was coming. Who doesn't, these days? I'm leaner and meaner myself. I don't think about that revolving door, spinning and spinning behind me, the sidewalk a new, wide-open space.

Maybe I'll write a book someday. The things I could tell. I get across the park – I walk uptown, so I come out at 90th Street – and already they're lining up to get into the Guggenheim Museum. The first time I saw this, I thought they must all be foreigners, but they're not. They're mostly Americans, and they come from New York, too.

I get another coffee from the stand parked on the corner. Seventy-five cents, which is too much. But it's fucking cold this morning. The wind hits my head and I wish I had a hat.

'Sandy!' Somebody comes up behind me and shouts in my ear. I'm not Sandy. I turn around, but the guy's not looking at me. Sandy's in line behind me, standing with her girlfriend.

She's cute. She's got short dark hair and a lot of lipstick, and red woollen mittens. The girlfriend's pretty cute too. I know, I know. But like I said, I'm a student of human nature. I can't help it.

'Art?' I think Sandy hasn't seen Art in a while. I step away and turn my back to them so I can listen.

'Hey, Sand, what's up? Long *time* no see. Nice to meet you –' he says to the other girl.

'Uh, Art, this is Felicia. Felicia, Art.'

'Nice to meet you, too.' This is the girlfriend talking. She doesn't sound convinced. There's this negative vibe coming off Sandy: I can feel it from here. But I think Art is oblivious.

'Doing the culture-vulture thing, huh? I guess the early bird catches the worm.' Art, master of the English language.

'Well, you know. We didn't think there'd be a line this early. Looks like everyone thought that.' She laughs. She's stuck, standing in line. It's Art that has to walk away. The coffee's terrible. I take another sip.

'Looks like it. But hey, did you get my message over the holidays? I left a couple on your machine but there were so many fuckin beeps I thought maybe it was on the fritz or something. I wanted to ask you about this new project that Steve's got going –'

'Steve?'

'Hey! Come on! Steve, Steve Bassett! He used to work at Dano's, remember? I know you remember. Anyway, he's got this new thing going at a gallery down on Spring – Canal? – Spring, I think – anyway, you know, conceptual, video, virtual reality, all that shit. The up and coming. We were having a few drinks the other night and he was laying it on me and I thought, Sand! This is Sandy's kind of thing! She's got to hear about this! And look at that, I run right into you here. It's karma, right?'

'Um... Art? I'm at law school now.' Her voice goes quiet. Lawyers, I guess, aren't into the conceptual shit.

'So I – you what? You're kidding.'

'No kidding. Columbia.' She's smiling now, I can hear it. She should be. She'll make a fucking ton.

'No shit. Hey. Good for you.' He blows into his hands and stamps. He's stuck. 'Well – I'll tell Steve. Maybe you'll come to the opening or something?'

'Right, Art. Leave me a message.' The line shuffles forward and their voices move a little farther away.

'I will, I will. Yeah, well. Anyway, good to see you, Sandy. Nice to meet you, Felicity.' His voice is a popped balloon. No shit, Art. Good morning. I drink my awful coffee through my teeth because I'm grinning. Art walks away.

'Fel*icity*,' Felicia says.

'Don't get me started. God, it's like shutting the vacuum cleaner off.'

'He's *your* friend. From under what rock?'

They're giggling like teenagers now. They're almost at the front of the line. I turn around and throw my cup in the trash. That Sandy has a cute ass on her too. Nothing like cold weather to get you thinking about women's asses.

I walk down Fifth, puffing into my scarf. This wind's coming down from Canada, I can tell you. It sucks the warmth right out of you and blows your hair to pieces. I keep pushing my hair out of my eyes and it just blows right back again.

That's when I think, I need a haircut. And I turn into this side street and what do you know, there's this barber pole right there. Karma, like Art said.

It's a weird place. A tiny little building all on its own, squashed between two huge expensive buildings, like a pebble stuck in a cliff face. It has a tin roof. I've never seen a tin roof in New York. The place is about the size of a bus, long and thin with one wall all mirrors, one of them cracked, and a border all around of coloured glass. I put my face on the cold glass and my breath steams the door. I can't see anyone. The floor is mottled black linoleum. It's seen better days, this place. But I like it. I rattle the door handle. The door's locked. I rattle it again and rap my knuckles on the glass.

An old man comes out of a door in the back. He's got a barber's smock on, snow white hair combed back just so and thick Buddy Holly glasses. He's holding a cup of something that steams. He gestures to me, pulling me in with his arm and smiling, and saying something that I can't hear. I rattle the door again and point to the knob. I make a big shrug with my shoulders like a clown. Fuck it's cold out here. Standing still makes me feel I just want to get inside, haircut or no haircut.

The old guy unlocks the door and I practically fall inside. My hair's all over the place. I can see his eyes, like fish in bowls through the thick lenses of his glasses, peering at it.

'I need a haircut.' I'm panting. It's so warm in here. It's nice.

'I can see,' he says. 'Have a seat.' He snaps a cape off a big old leather barber chair with a ringmaster's flourish. His fat little finger has a thick gold ring on it. I go to sit down and then I remember.

'How much?'

'Cut and shave?'

'Just a cut.'

He's staring at my chin now. But there's nothing I can do.

'Twelve dollars fifty cents.' He's got this little accent. Italian, maybe. I read once that all the good barbers are Italian. I'm in luck. But twelve fifty. That's steep for me. And I've only got three and a quarter now. But I don't care. I've got to have this haircut. A man needs a haircut. What's Lin going to think if I start coming home with my hair all over my ears, curling down my collar like a dead man's?

'I've got to go get some cash,' I say. 'I'll be right back. Hold the chair.'

'Yes sir,' he says. He doesn't smile. He's what I guess you'd call grave, like he takes all this very seriously. I head out the door and the freezing wind attacks my head again.

There's a bank on the corner of Madison. I keep my cash card in the back of my wallet now, behind all the old receipts and dog-eared business cards ('Here – can I give you my card?') so I have to hunt for it in the wind. Someone stands behind me. A man in a suit, a man like me.

'Sorry.'

He grimaces at me and I assume it's a smile. The

brotherhood of men. Don't look now, buddy, you're next, is what I think.

The card slips into the machine with a smooth sexy click. I do everything the machine tells me to do but when it flashes my balance on the little screen I look away. Once a month I make myself look. But today I just ask for twenty dollars and the machine offers me two new tens. I slip them in my wallet, no big deal. I used to take out a hundred at a time, sometimes two. I wonder how much Smiler behind me takes. I walk away and we nod at each other, ships in the night. So long, pal.

The barber's waiting for me. Opens the door and ushers me in, reaches up to take my coat from my shoulders. He's really very short. But stocky, like you wouldn't want to mess with him. When I get in the chair he has to pump it right down so he can reach my head.

And there's my face in the big mirror right in front of me. Long time no see. I smile at myself. I stare. I forget that the little guy's watching me. I try to figure out how different I look. I'm looking for lines. I see them, but I'm sure they were there before. It's not so bad. I smile again. I've got good teeth. I've always been proud of my teeth.

'Mister.'

I jump like I've just woken up.

'What you want?'

Jesus, my heart is going in my chest. 'Short back and sides. Just short back and sides.' I talk to him in the mirror. He nods and pushes his heavy glasses up on his nose. There's a long skinny scissors on the cluttered shelf in front of me, the real old barber's kind with a tail coming off one of the loop handles, and he picks these up and shoots his cuff. His pinky, the one with the ring, rests on the tail. He takes up a thin black plastic comb. Then he takes my chin in his right hand, puts his left on the back of my head, tips my head forward and gets to work.

When I was a kid I used to hate to have my hair cut. My mother used to take me to her hairdresser, out in Brooklyn, where we lived, and one of the girls would cut my hair. Sitting with my neck bent over, staring at my shoes I can still smell the hairspray stink of the place. The girls had sharp red fingernails that always seemed to catch in my ears and I hated the bright pink smock they wrapped around me. I used to keep my eyes shut the whole time. It was humiliating. 'Time for a cut, honey,' my mom would say, pushing my bangs out of my eyes, and my stomach would shrink right up inside me. What was I afraid of? That one of my friends would see me. And of course one of them did. Just once, but it was enough. Jimmy goes to the beauty parlor. I tell you, I never thought I'd live that down. It was why I grew my hair in college. I wasn't any kind of beatnik. It was just such a relief not to have my hair cut.

But I got over it. And this is OK. The barber puts his fingers under my chin again and lifts my head so I can look at myself again. I can't see any difference, he's just been going at the back. There's a Christmas card propped by the mirror, a big one, with green holly and red berries. It's a little open. To Frank, it says, Thanks and Happy New Year. Next to it there's an old framed photograph of a guy with swept-back black hair and Buddy Holly glasses and a serious face, standing outside a building, maybe a school. Is it the barber? Frank, the barber? I turn my eyes back and forth between the picture and Frank (maybe Frank is someone else, the barber's partner, but I'm pretty sure this is Frank behind me). It's hard to tell. You'd think it would be easy but the picture is like a thousand others from thirty years ago. It could be my Dad. He had glasses like that. I think everybody did. I want to ask the barber if it's him but his serious face stops me. He's concentrating on my hair and that's good. He takes my hair between his fingers and frowns at it and snips, very fast, and the little hairs fall like rain on my shoulders.

There's a heater right by my feet and waves of hot air waft up the legs of my pants. A month ago I'd have asked him to turn it off – 'It cracks the leather of my shoes' – but a month is a longer time than you think. I settle into the heat and close my eyes and listen to the cheep, cheep of the scissors and the hum of Fifth and the heater like an ancient cat. He pulls a comb through my hair and snips, and pulls it through and snips, working back from my forehead and I can feel my head getting lighter and my mind clearer. It's a dead weight. When I'm gone he'll sweep my hair into a pan and throw it in the trash. He leaves me with only what I need. I open my eyes. He's watching my head in the mirror to see how I look. He's a student of human nature too.

'OK?'

'Great.'

'This way, please.' He puts the scissors down, tips my head again, just this way – no, just that – and reaches into his pocket. Christ. I didn't think they made those things anymore. It's a

114

straight razor. I stare ahead into the mirror. He adjusts his glasses on his nose and I hear a noise, whisht, whisht, whisht as he sharpens the razor on a leather strop that hangs off the back of the chair and which I never noticed before. He blows on the blade and regards it in the dull white light like he's a surgeon.

'Just this way.' His fingers cup my chin and stretch the skin of my cheek. The cold razor rasps beside my ear, like a cat's tongue. I've never sat so still in my life before. I don't look in the mirror but at the cracked counter in front of me, which is all covered in little hairs of all different colours, like the linoleum below. It isn't very clean. I start to think about AIDS.

But then I remember it's Frank with the razor in his hand. Frank's an artist. I relax a little and he tips my head the other way and does the other sideburn, pressing on my face so I can feel my jawbone underneath. We both look at me in the mirror. It's a good haircut. It's sharp.

'Just natural, at the back?'

'Just natural, yeah.'

He tips me forward again and the razor catches the light, flashing in the mirror. It's so sharp that all I feel on my skin is cold, nothing else, while his left hand holds me steady. His fingers smell of flowers and are warm and dry, pressing gently on my forehead and holding me still and safe while the cut-throat brushes the tight skin over my spine. The thought I have at this moment is that I've never felt anything so good as his warm, sure fingers, that I never want to leave this shop. The thought is so strange and new that it makes me tremble, and for a second I'm afraid he'll cut me. But he won't. He won't.

Jamie

He has a dream of speed. Very early in the morning, when the light has barely begun, he lies on his back beside his wife, his toes stretched down to the bottom of the bed and a corner of the sheet a damp ball in his fist. Beneath his closed lids his eyes quiver, senseless as embryos, as tadpoles. He breathes through his nose, loudly, though his wife doesn't wake. She turns on her side, to the window, and settles into her pillow again.

He is racing. He is behind the wheel of a racing car, those strange splayed machines that whine endlessly around tracks on the telly. Sometimes, on a Saturday, he'll flick past the racing and then back again. Watch it, just for a moment. If Ellen is in the room he will say, 'I don't know what anyone sees in it,' and then move on, before turning the box off completely and raising the newspaper again. Ellen will agree with him, and go back out to the garden. And he doesn't know what anyone sees in it, except that in his dreams here he is, his arms straight out in front of him, his head encased in a helmet whose visor clouds with his breath. He can smell it, his breath: it is tainted with metal, with his fear. He has never done this before and yet he knows that something awesome depends on the outcome of this race, that perhaps his life depends on it, or Ellen's. He can see no other drivers. Perhaps he is winning. His body is rattled by the power of the car, the ground is uneven and makes his joints pound into each other. He is beginning to have arthritis: it hurts. But still he holds the wheel, and follows the black snake of the tarmac as it spools out ahead of him. He takes one turn, and then another, and then despite the pain in his hips and knees and the terrible roaring, like a thousand lions, in his ears, he begins to believe he will reach the finish. It is a checkered flag, he knows this much. And in his dream it is this conviction, that it might be possible for him to succeed, that makes him lose his grip on the wheel and feel the car slip and fishtail out and flip over as it hits the edge of the tarmac. He sees the ground, now beneath him, very clearly, and upside down the high side wall of the track for which he is heading, very slowly and with infinite speed, and against which his bones will shatter. He smells the ignition, the beginning of the flame.

When he wakes up he stands by the window and looks out at the creeping dawn.

Jamie is home from college: they go for a drink at the pub. Ellen looks at her watch as they leave, a small watch on her widening wrist, a gold watch that Simon gave her when they had been married twenty years. She had laughed, 'For good service!' Now she says, 'be back in time for dinner. Eight o'clock.'

They walk easily together, father and son, their strides fitting like soldiers' so there is only the sound of one person walking on the quiet suburban streets. They don't speak. Jamie has his mother's curly hair, his father's deep-set eyes: he is their marriage made flesh. Simon remembers poring over the body of his tiny son, nineteen years ago and more, searching for the signs of himself, the witness to his own existence. Now it walks beside him in the blue twilight.

Here is the sign of The Blue Ball: a woman bent over her crystal globe, a turban on her head and clustered around her shoulders like birds the wondering faces of children. Her hands, beringed, spread out in front of her magic glass, and her mouth is a round O. True to its name the ball sheds blue light which throws cold upward shadows, signifiers of surprise or fear. The sign swings in the warm wind. The paint is beginning to peel, ageing the children into elves or leprechauns. What do they see? The future or the past? When Simon opens the door a streak of gold spills out onto the ground.

Noisy. 'What'll you have?' and he puts his hand on his son's shoulder, feeling the blade of bone beneath his jumper like a wing.

'Guinness.'

Simon shouts for two pints and brings the black columns of liquid back to where Jamie has seated himself. In a corner, his face a little in shadow, dipped away from the light as he rolls a cigarette.

'There you go.'

Jamie nods with the pink tip of his tongue resting on his upper lip, pulling the Rizla against it. He finds matches in the pocket of his

119

*jacket, lights the thin twist of paper and puffs. He lifts his pint.
'Thanks, Dad.'*

*Simon feels pleasure rise like heat in his face at his son's simple
words. Mostly Simon doesn't mind the silences between them. The
silences happen because Simon does not often know what Jamie would
say. Simon can speak of his own life, but what will his son answer? It
is a mystery. It is enough to look at him, his fine clear face, ruddy in
the cheeks like Simon used to be.*

*Simon drinks the bitter froth off his glass and Jamie rises, counting
the coins in his palm. By the door of the pub is a game, a racing game
with a stumpy black wheel and a screen, on which a road unfolds endlessly in the distance, all around the flat plain of the world. Jamie feeds
his coins into the game and it makes a noise, an explosion. Simon
watches the muscles in his son's neck. Jamie grips the wheel. Jamie rests
his foot on the accelerator pedal, ignores the brake, drives his imagination along the ribbon of road, his back jerking and twitching like
something filled with electricity. Through the crook of Jamie's arm
Simon can just see the hairpin video bends, the high side walls of the
track. Sweat beads between his eyes. He wipes it away quickly. It is
only make-believe. He looks at his watch. It is almost dinner time.
Simon gets up from the table and leaves the two pint glasses, one
empty, one full, to be cleared away.*

Dressing for work, Simon stands at the bedroom window,
watching Ellen in the garden. It is a large garden, with a little
pond and three pear trees. It is the reason they bought this
house. She is walking around its perimeter with a trug slung
over her forearm and a secateurs in her hand, observing the

roses in the morning light. She lifts their heavy heads gently in her fingers, turns them to the sun, examines them, strokes their velvety petals with the ball of her thumb. Every so often she inserts the secateurs in the thick of a bush, and he hears a distant click. She lays the rose gently in her basket, Pharoah's daughter with Moses. When she has gathered enough, she will arrange them simply in the heavy crystal vase on the mantle: by the time he gets home from work their festival scent will have filled the house.

At the bottom of the garden is the shed where Ellen works. Ellen's shed is solid and snug, built with close-fitting clapboards and a foundation of rough concrete; it has two large windows and is wired for electricity. A tall oil cylinder, like a sentry, stands against its back. This is a fine shed. Inside is Ellen's wheel and her kiln (it is this that burns the oil), her plastic bins of clay with their sweet wet scent, the magic colourbox of her glazes. Ellen started with a pottery course, an evening class for ladies – well, there were only ladies there – with nothing better to do, but over the years she has surprised herself and Simon by becoming a potter. She has a reputation. Sometimes – it happens more often now, maybe once a month, more in the summer – people knock on their front door and ask to see her pots. They buy them. Ellen names a figure snatched from the air while Simon stands in the doorway of the kitchen, smiling, proud, embarrassed by his surprise.

When the visitors have gone she will be flushed and happy, standing on the threshold to watch them drive away. Simon will take her hands in his and kiss them. They are useful hands: they look older than the rest of her, ingrained as they are with clay in every line and pore. They smell of soil, as if they were the branching roots of saplings pulled up growing from the earth.

Later she will go back to her shed, her studio. The wheel is still. She builds a pot with a coil of clay, rolling the red stuff into a shapely snake and winding it around on itself, building a fine base, a swelling belly, a living container for wine, for life, for what you please. But it doesn't satisfy. When it is still wet she smashes it with her fist, pounding it hard to push out the air that will otherwise become trapped in the clay and make it crack when it is fired. These bubbles of breath, deadly to the animate earth. She rocks against her collapsed pot, slapping it, throwing it, making it whole again, a solid lump of itself. The red clay warms to the heat of her blood as she digs her strong fingers into its flesh and stares at nothing, through her table, through the floor, through the concrete and compacted earth beneath her feet, rocking and rocking with the clay, and Simon doesn't know that she will do this for hours sometimes, or that tears will streak out from under the rims of her glasses, shining eels she does not control. They fall on her hands and make the clay slippery and useless. She will wipe her face with her dirty hands, make tea, stand in the sunny garden.

Simon also does not know of the creatures that live beside the kiln, beneath her table by the wall of the shed. Little clay elves, *putti*, lumpy babies not quite human, clearly of the earth from which they are formed. She makes them – she hardly knows how often. When the mood takes her. She builds them from her coloured clays, moulding their hollowed bodies and curled foetal limbs, and shaping their ugly faces with her hands, smiling as she works. She likes to make the faces. These aren't happy children: they howl, they wail, their small mouths are stretched in agony as if they might be damned, and all because she makes them so. She fires their frozen grimaces into permanence. She allows them to accumulate until there are too many to cower beneath her table, and then she will smash them, early in the morning, just after Simon is gone. It does not cause her any pain to smash them. She does it with a hammer. It is, in fact, satisfying. And then she will begin again.

After they have had supper, Simon does the washing-up while Ellen sits at the cleared table with a cup of coffee and the paper. Simon dries the dishes (a wedding present, not made by Ellen) and puts things away carefully in the pretty glass-fronted kitchen cupboards. He is proud of the fact (though he would not admit this to anyone) that after more than twenty years of marriage they still have every single piece of their wedding china. Not one cup, not one saucer, has been smashed on the hard tile floor. He attributes this to his own innate caution – Ellen has been known to call him fussy – and Ellen's care of anything made of earth. Ten years ago Ellen lost his mother's pearl necklace (Simon remembers this, how could he not? but he does not hold it against her), but china she will not break.

Wiping his hands on a towel he kisses the top of her head as she bends over her newspaper. Her crown sprouts with grey. Has it been so long? He is amazed.

'I'm going upstairs,' he says. 'Just some notes to tidy up.'

Simon is the executive director of a small specialized firm which manufactures glass for scientific instruments. Simon is good at his job and the firm is successful. His fussiness serves him well. Often, in the evenings, there will be accounts to go over, annual reports to peruse, his hands always lightly on the reins. He enjoys his work.

But once upstairs in his study he doesn't open his black briefcase. He moves it from his desk and sets it on the floor. Instead he finds a sheet of writing paper in the bottom drawer of his desk, holds his pen up to the light to see that it still contains ink, and sits down. The sheet of paper in front of him is an expensive cream colour, thick and fine, and it pools out before him like an expectant still pond. He lifts his pen.

Dear Jamie,

It was very good to see you last weekend. Your mother and I are so pleased at how you're getting on at college – Mum says she'd only be worried if you wanted to come home all the time! And we appreciate the journey is a 'hassle'. But you know you must always feel free to come, even without a call before, and if you ever want to bring anyone, that's fine too.

Simon tries to push himself into these stiff words, to make them sound like himself. Or at least to make them sound like the father he wishes to be: firm but relaxed, full of advice (given only when requested) that is sound, never patriarchal; easygoing about girlfriends and money. He recollects his own father, fount of bombast and admonitions: not like that.

Mum sold another pot just after you left – the tall yellowish amphora that was sitting by the fireplace. A young couple passing through, just about to have a baby, they'd heard about Mum from a friend, they said. The word of mouth is quite impressive. Mum's thinking of going down to Cornwall in the summer, there's a crafts fair there –

And of course Jamie is always interested in what he has to tell him. It's easier for Jamie, Simon thinks, reading a letter, in his own time, not having to compose his face like he does in the pub, at the dinner table: no father is the perfect father at a certain stage of life and Simon appreciates this. Which is why he writes the letters. He knows in his heart that Jamie is glad to get them.

– and I might go too if I can get a week off. We might take a cottage, who knows? You could come too – I do remember you paddling in the sea when

This is ridiculous. He crosses it out.

You could come too, if you wanted, if you don't mind being with your old parents for a whole week. As I said, you're always welcome.

Is this too much? But he can't help himself. His love for his son squeezes his heart and flows out of his pen like it is his own blood. He begins to write faster and faster, spilling out the memories he holds in his head, memories so vivid they blind him like a veil across his sight.

Do you remember

Turned into words, no matter how awkward, they become solid things, the matter of his life, like bricks, like clay, the proof of himself laid out on to sheets and sheets of costly paper, kept in the bottom drawer of his desk like a shameful secret, a kind of pornography.

Do you remember

His hand cramps and his vision blurs but still he writes, on and on, blinking away the prism that threatens to explode the neat black lines of his being. When he reaches the bottom of the fourth sheet something inside him withers. His back sinks. Here he is at his desk. The pen has rubbed a hard red spot on the second finger of his right hand. It is nearly ten o'clock and soon Ellen will ask if he wants a cup of tea.

Slowly and carefully he takes the four pages he has written, aligns them, folds them in three, and slides them neatly into an envelope of the same rich cream paper. This he puts in the bottom drawer of his desk, alongside his stationery, and then he goes downstairs.

★

Once every fortnight Simon and Ellen drive to Ellen's parents, who live in a town not far away, an hour if the traffic is good. They are hale and hearty, Ellen's parents, they are all the words that are used of old people whose younger acquaintances expect them to be dead: going strong, tough as old boots, a few good years left yet. They live in a small tidy terraced house which always smells of polish and something roasting (Simon and Ellen come for lunch) and Simon always watches with fascination and with envy the spectacle of Ellen's elderly parents greeting and embracing their daughter, their only child, now herself a woman growing older, a woman with grey hairs.

Simon drives there. Ellen, forsaking a second glass of wine, drives back. This has the force of ritual. Once, about five years ago, Ellen turned to Simon in the car (on the way there: he was at the wheel) and said, 'You don't mind this, do you?'

'What?'

'Going to see my parents. Every fortnight.'

'No,' he said. Quite automatically. And then he thought about it. 'No. I don't.' And that was how he really felt. That was the end of that.

So every fortnight they go, and every fortnight almost the same sequence of not much happens. The greeting, the shrugging off of coats (if it is winter), the little glass of dry sherry, a comment on the weather. Ellen retreats with her mother into the kitchen, and Simon stays in the sitting-room with Ellen's father, taking the other armchair. They talk about football or cricket, and sometimes they talk about the markets with more confidence than either of them feels. The vast gaps in their dis-course, the holes which open blackly and suddenly like crevasses in ice, could so easily be mistaken for ordinary silence, the gentle pauses that naturally occur between people of long-standing acquaintance. Simon and his father-in-law do not acknowledge these silences. This is the rule of the family, and Simon accepts it although he is unaware of how it came to be. The rule holds Simon in a kind of awed fascination.

'More sherry?' Ellen's father stands up, leans toward the bottle on the sideboard, on one of these ceaseless Sundays, a Sunday like any other.

'I'm all right, thanks.' So Ellen's father – William – pours himself another, just a half, his back to his son-in-law.

Which is when Simon notices a black-backed book on the piano bench, something thick and bound in mock-leather and which he has not noticed before. Simon prides himself on the noticing of details. He picks it up without any sense of intru-sion, without any notion of himself as nosy. He is not nosy. It is lying out on the piano bench. This is the home of his wife's parents, a home he knows almost as well as his own.

It is, of course, a photo album. And there on the first page – and on the second, and the third, and after that as well, is Jamie. Little Jamie, less than two, standing uncertainly on wobbly legs and peering into the unfamiliar eye of the camera, his skin gone a pale mushroom colour as the cheap print has faded, his face shadowed, squinting and sour. Turn the page. Now smiling, in close up, indoors, in his eyes the orange glare of a flashbulb. Pages and pages, all Jamie, all Jamie, these pictures that Simon has not seen in he does not know how long, Jamie stopped, only a baby, never more than that.

'Simon.'

William has turned around. Simon looks up and sees that his father-in-law has gone the same mushroom colour that he sees in the pictures. William thrusts his hands out, asking for the book, hoping to retract his terrible mistake, to hide the thing away, to pillow his head once more in the down of the blessed silence.

'Dinner's ready,' sings his mother-in-law – Ruth – as she enters the room followed by her smiling daughter.

Simon holds the shining pages of the book between his fingers, stroking their cool surfaces. 'He's getting on quite well now,' Simon hears his own voice like an echo inside his head. It pushes out of his mouth, escaping steam, a volcano, vomit. 'He's doing well. At college. Don't you think?'

Before he could stop himself. In front of their astonished faces. His words alone make the life of his son, Jamie, killed by a careless driver just before his second birthday. His words make Jamie stand in front of them, a man, a young man who loves his father, who reads the letters his father writes him, a fine young man who will watch his father grow old.

A Simple Question

Nous voulons – I said. *Nous avons desirées* – but I couldn't get out much more. There were so many of them, swarming around me like ants, one of them, a woman, caressing my limbs, kneading me as if I were delicate pastry: her cool hands through my clothing were soothing and unearthly, and I must have leaned back against her because when she stopped I nearly fell. They all rushed to catch me, hats askew, faces swollen and strange in the pulsing blue light. The police radios crackled and snapped. Someone spoke English, was trying to talk to me, but I clung doggedly to the construction of half-remembered verbs. Freya's French is very good, she is always the one to order the food and ask directions. My French was better, once. As she wasn't there just then, I thought I should take advantage of the opportunity to practise.

★

I had wanted Freya's bicycle. I was nine. I wanted it so badly I dreamed about it. It's not that I didn't have a bike: I did, handed down to me from our neighbour's daughter across the street, a purple bicycle with wide white tires, a flowered banana seat and those enormous handlebars, shaped like the horns of Highland cattle, with plastic tassels at the ends. I was never not embarrassed by that bicycle. I rode it all right, and I don't think I complained, but when I'd had it about a year my best friend got a new bicycle for her birthday, and after that I knew no rest.

Freya's bicycle was a real bicycle, with thin black wheels, spanking silver paint, drop handlebars, a narrow seat and a French name up the side. It had gears, and brakes you had to work with your hands, and not a tassle in sight. Her father wheeled it out to her on the morning of her birthday – it was a Saturday, so I had slept over – and it glowed in the sunlight of the breakfast room like the Holy Grail. It was the most beautiful thing I had ever seen. She let me ride it, of course: she even let me ride it first. I circled it slowly round their driveway, wobbling uncertainly: it was queer to be crouched down low over those sinuous, serious handlebars after having sat up so straight on my battered old bike. It was hard to reach the brakes. But I didn't care. I loved it all the same. Covetousness suffused my blood like a drug.

I suffered that particular sin a great deal when I was around Freya: I got in the habit of wanting early on. Freya's parents, to put it bluntly, were loaded: Freya had everything there was to have. I don't think she thought anything about it; for her that was the way the world worked.

It was not the way the world worked for me. Freya and I went to the same fancy East Side school, but my parents, as they say, made sacrifices to send me there. My uniforms were second-hand, just like my bicycle, and my shirts didn't have little animals stitched carefully on to the pockets. I was never deprived – only, I was always just a little aware that there was a life I was missing. I think I knew very early on that this was not a noble notion, and I tried very hard not to ask for things I knew I would never get. But I talked about that bicycle a lot. I came home from the weekend of Freya's birthday – we had spent it out at their country house on Long Island – and sat at the dinner table with my parents, describing the wonders of the incredible machine. I curled my hands in the air to make the shape of its handlebars; I held my arms in a graceful hoop to show the size of its wheels.

'Sounds like some bike,' Dad said, looking at me in a way he had, which let me know that he knew what I was thinking, and that it was all right by him.

'It is, Dad. It's amazing.'

The bicycle took its place at the table, an uninvited guest.

My mother watched my father with wary eyes. 'More chicken?' she asked, and that was the end of that.

But on Christmas morning, I got a bicycle, a brand new bicycle, a bicycle just like Freya's.

When we got to the station, I finally stopped trying to pile participle onto participle and let the policeman who spoke English ask me questions. He was a nice man, with a soft face like a bassett hound's that looked like it had spent too many nights like this, questioning crazy foreign women at three o'clock in the morning. His name was Renault, like the car. While we talked, he took my fingerprints. He held my fingers as if they were newts and pressed them down firmly on a pad of ink, then pressed them again on cards that said *main gauche* and *main droite*. He talked to me all the while, as if he didn't want me to notice what he was doing. A policewoman – I guess she spoke English too, although she never opened her mouth – sat behind me and took notes. He wouldn't let me talk about what happened. Begin at the beginning, he said. I didn't know where to start.

'Tell me your name.'

'Suzanne Jenson,' I said. 'Suzanne Ryan Jenson.' It was, still.

'And – your friend?'

'Yes, my friend. Freya Morgan.'

'You are on holiday here, in Arles?'

'Yes – well, in Avignon. We're staying in Avignon.'

He was finished fingerprinting me. He gave me a cloth to wipe my blackened hands, and snapped the inkpad shut. Then he rubbed his face hard with his hands, as if it were wet and he was washing it, and the loose skin of his mouth made a flapping noise against his gums. 'Would you like a coffee, Mrs Jenson?'

'Ms,' I said quickly. It made a nasty buzz in my mouth, hissing at him. I saw his glance catch the gold on my left hand, but he nodded and began again.

'Would you like a coffee, Mizz Jenson?' One eyebrow,

134

slightly arched. My throat felt tight. There were mistakes to make. I would not recognize them.

'Yes please,' I said.

He scribbled something on a pad; he looked into my eyes; and then shaped his ink-stained, hang-dog face into a mask of concern as he asked me questions, question after question, about Freya, about me, about the two of us together. I told him Freya and I had come on holiday together to Avignon. It was her idea. You have to get away, she had said. You have to get out of this apartment. It was a small apartment, just over the bridge in Brooklyn, and I had told Bart to leave it. I hadn't explained the reason why to him very well, but he had gone anyway. Maybe that was worse. Freya had packed my bag. She was still my best friend. I'm taking you away, she said. Let's go.

She paid for the tickets, booked the hotel. She's the youngest partner in the history of her firm. She folded my shirts and held the phone under her chin, explaining, delegating, arranging, using words I'd never heard. I work for myself. It doesn't matter what I do. It's easy to leave. We went.

He let me talk and talk. I told him everything that wasn't important in an effort to find out what was. Finally I wasn't listening to what I was saying anymore. It was easy enough to recite the stories I knew, to tell him about the parking ticket we got in Orange and the terrible meal in Les Baux, while my mind was somewhere else.

I was thinking that all my life I'd got everything I ever wanted. I had a knack for it. It started with that bicycle and grew from there like a cancer, unstoppable. One after another things fell into my lap, manna from heaven, and I collected them with increasing dissatisfaction. Possessions, boyfriends, university degrees. And Bart, of course, whom I had wanted most of all. After a while I hadn't wanted him, and he'd gone. That was what I'd wanted too.

Freya was there to pick up the pieces. She always was. She knew best.

The policewoman handed Renault her notes, and he looked them over. I could just see that she had written everything in French.

Then another policeman brought the coffee on a tray. There were two cups, one for Renault and one for me, and when mine was set down in front of me I said *merci* to the officer, who was very tall and very young and looked as if his uniform was brand new.

'That's OK,' he said, and smiled.

Every morning, for the seven days we were in Avignon, Freya and I used to walk out of our hotel across the Place d'Horloge to a big sunny cafe on the other side of the square. We'd buy the *Herald Tribune* and split it in half and order coffee. I'd have mine with hot milk, and I would drop in three of those little sugar lumps and watch them fizz in the creamy liquid. Freya liked her coffee black. *Et un noir, double,* she would say. Her coffee was a dark oily smudge in the bottom of the cup, rimmed with tawny foam.

That was the sort of coffee they brought me. The smell was sharp and sour and it was black as a hole in the ground. Renault sat back in his chair, cradled his cup in his palm and said: 'Now, Mizz Jenson, would you like to tell me what you and your friend were doing in the amphitheatre at two o'clock in the morning?'

I stared down into my coffee and started to cry.

It was the first week of January, and Freya and her parents and her two little brothers were just back from skiing when I got to take my bike, my amazing bike, up to their house on Long Island. The Morgans' car had a rack on the roof and her father strapped it on: the whole way up I was terrified it would shake itself loose, or blow off, but it didn't, and when we pulled into their gravelled driveway and got out it reared like a charger, straining against the cords that bound it to the dark-green Mercedes.

There was a light dusting of snow on the ground, and Long Island Sound stretched away in the distance, grey and choppy with cold. The Morgans' house was on a bluff high above the water, and miles from anyone else. It was an enormous place, built by a millionaire in the fifties, a single-storeyed snake of a house that seemed to wind for miles, doubling back on itself and sprouting rooms with too many walls: pentagons, hexagons, octagons. It was easy to lose your bearings and get lost. There were whole walls made of glass and every room had a bubble skylight: at night the trees would blow and scrape against these, and the leaves would press their pale undersides against the rounded panes. In winter Freya and I could lie awake and watch the snow fall and clump like knotted lace.

Mr Morgan handed the bike down to me with great care. I took it from him and leaned on the handlebars with what I imagined was an air of nonchalance. Freya had already run into the garage to get her own bike, and wheeled it out towards me.

'Come on, Suzy, let's go,' she said. She looked at her mother, who nodded and said, 'But be back in an hour. I'll be making lunch.'

'Okay, Mom.'

'Thanks, Mrs Morgan,' I said. Mrs Morgan made grilled cheese for lunch. It was the only thing she could cook. They had a housekeeper. Mrs Morgan had been a model. Sometimes I wished she was my mother, but not at lunchtime.

Freya could get on her bike by rolling it forward and hopping, one foot on one pedal, until she'd got enough speed to swing her other long leg up over the saddle and down, and she did that now, gliding away down the drive, leaning low over the handlebars, up off the saddle, her hips rising and falling as she began to pedal. I followed, hurriedly, awkwardly: getting my leg over the crossbar, jumping up and down, leaning the bike to get myself on to the saddle, catching a pedal with my toe.

'Coming?' Freya yelled from the bottom of the drive.

'Coming –' My heart was jolting in my chest but finally I was away, pedals spinning because I wasn't about to change gear, feeling a very long way from the ground. It was at that moment, I think, that I started to miss my gentle purple bike with its flowered banana seat.

Freya always stayed just ahead. I spent a lot of time behind her, those weekends in the country. I guess I was proud of her assumption that I could always keep up, but I never could. Later, Freya would play centre for the basketball team and win the Interschool women's high jump two years in a row. Such glories were not destined for me.

But I would not be beaten by a bicycle. By a bicycle that I ought, by rights, to have loved more than anything in the world, but which I was quickly growing to loathe as its sleek skinny wheels wobbled on the frosty road. There was a grinding noise, and a jerking – I wagged the front wheel back and forth in alarm but managed to retain my balance – and the bike changed gear of its own accord. I was relieved. It made it easier to pedal. Freya became less distant.

'How're you doing?' she called.

'Just great,' I shouted, very loudly so she'd think I was even closer than I was.

The wind bit into the skin of my face as it came hard off the sea. The naked trees dripped with ice, although perhaps that is a detail I note only in memory: at the time my mind was pretty well occupied by my bike, my desire, the possibility of failure, and success as close as the next dip in the road. The roads themselves were narrow and twisting, and unpredictably hilly: driving on them – Mr Morgan always drove fast – you rose up and down in your seat, your stomach always following just a little behind, like on the Cyclone at Coney Island. The red reflector on the back of Freya's saddle hung just ahead of me. We were going uphill now; my thighs grew heavy and bloodless with the effort.

At the crest of the hill I looked up. There was a big trawler in the Sound, white wings of waves breaking against her bows. I almost came to a stop, but just when I didn't think I could pedal anymore the downhill took my bike and started to pull it towards the sea.

I lost my head. I started to backpedal to brake, but nothing happened: the chain clicked and the pedals spun and my feet flew off at right angles and the bike swayed like a ship in a storm. We were gathering speed at a tremendous rate, bombing down the hill, the wind so strong I thought my eyelids would blow off. I couldn't remember where the brakes were. The trees, the road, the sea blurred into a noisy grey galloping nothingness that swallowed up the world.

The bike wasn't too badly damaged. The handlebars were bent and some spokes were knocked in. Both tyres went flat. We had parted company soon in what was, according to Freya (who had heard a strange noise and turned around) a spectacular fall, and I had skidded on my face for what felt like several miles before grinding to a halt near the bottom of the hill. My wrist was broken and my two front teeth were gone, and I had gravel embedded in my skin like terrible blackheads. I think Freya carried me back to the house, but I don't really remember. I remember the hospital though, and the dentist. To this day I'm nervous about biting into apples, and I cut my sweetcorn off the cob.

Freya and I were in the fourth grade that winter. After the accident we seemed to take it for granted, both of us, that there were things that Freya was good at and that I was not.

There didn't seem to be any that worked the other way. We were best friends.

My father fixed the handlebars and the spokes on the bike, and it looked almost as good as new. But I never rode it again.

Renault tapped a short, thick cigarette out of a pack and offered it to me, just like in the movies. I shook my head. He took it himself, and lit it, and blew out a cloud of bitter brown smoke.

'You were aware that the amphitheatre is closed to the public after six o'clock in the evening? There is, I believe, a locked gate at every entrance.'

'Yes,' I said. 'We saw the gates. And the locks. But they're pretty rickety. We squeezed through.'

'So it would appear.'

His face, which at first had seemed kind and thoughtful to me, looked less so now. Hard lines ran down its length, creased his forehead, like grooves cut in wood. I sensed he would be quick to scorn and easily disappointed: he was certainly disappointed in me.

On our seventh night in the Hotel Florale, Freya and I lay on our backs under the starched sheets, still as effigies. Our room had one wide, double bed. Freya had asked for a twin, but there had been some confusion – upon our arrival the slight, dark proprietress had sighed and wrung her gold-ringed hands, her blunt nails perfectly manicured, the sharp line of her black hair trembling against her chin. *Pardonnez-moi, Mademoiselles*, she said. *Pardonnez-moi*. It didn't matter. We didn't mind.

The window was open. A warm breeze blew through the net curtain, whispering like voices in an adjoining room. The hotel was small, in a back street, with little high-ceilinged rooms made fortresses by their great wooden shutters. I was glad that Freya had chosen this place, not some bland, business-trip Intercontinental. At the airport she had rented a car and driven me here, and I had let myself be taken by her, uncomplaining, barely asking where we were going or what we were doing. I was tired of decisions. The ease of Bart's going had sucked the strength out of me, as if my power to make him go had gone with him and left me hollow, not wanting him but wanting something, always something, puzzled by the Bart-shaped hole that seemed to have been left inside me. We had been married five years. We had no children. I had taken his name. Suzanne Jenson. Suzanne Ryan was far away, out of focus.

I had not imagined that on this trip Freya and I would sit up through the night, chewing down our lives into word-size pieces. Freya wasn't like that. She wasn't much of a talker (she must have been an unusual lawyer). When we were girls together, sometimes we'd spend whole weekends in each others' company and hardly say a word. It was easy. It seemed – companionable. She had led and I had followed. Here we were again. She had driven us south, from Lyons airport, through the bright yellow French morning, quiet, both hands on the wheel, her hazel eyes straight ahead. I had turned to watch her. She didn't mind, or didn't notice. Her face was strong, not beautiful, really, with a high forehead, a long nose. Her thick brown hair pulled back in a ponytail. She was still athletic, she still skied, and when she shifted gear I could see the muscles in her thigh flex as she dropped the clutch.

But then, this seventh night, the moon threw cool shadows around the room and wouldn't let us sleep. Freya turned on her side, the sheet smooth over her hip like a fall of powder snow. 'What are you thinking?' she asked.

It wasn't like her. 'About today,' I said. 'How beautiful it was. Seeing the city from up high like that.'

We had driven – she had driven – to Arles. We had parked by the main square and walked, past all the sites so carefully detailed in our slim green schoolmistress of a guidebook, down to the river where we had found a funfair erupting on the banks. We hadn't been to any funfairs. We had been to abbeys and vineyards and temples and churches, we had read aloud in turns from our guide, we had walked for miles. Freya led the way. I did not know her plan and I did not ask, but if I had to guess I would have said she was trying to erase my image of Bart by layering it over with the lavender and gold tissue of Provence.

Here it was different. The air, thick with the smell of burnt sugar, sausages, cigarette smoke, shivered with acid pinks and greens. In front of us was an enormous Ferris wheel, revolving slowly against the bleached sky like a slowly turning galaxy, lit with coloured star-lights and hung with dozens of swaying seats.

'Let's go on it,' I said.

Freya didn't turn to look at me. 'I thought you didn't like heights,' she said.

'No,' I said. 'That was just Bart. Bart was tall. I didn't like him.'

She laughed at that, and I did too, and things seemed simple again. We walked quickly to the ticket booth and I bought two tickets. We stood in line and then climbed into our little seat, and then through the awful organ-grinder music we began to rise and rise, watching the city sink beneath us, its red-tiled roofs and winding streets framed in the dirty white girders of the wheel.

The amphitheatre dominated the city, a huge open mouth gaping at the sky, its throat filled with tourists. It was Easter; it was very crowded. I don't like that kind of crowd, but I wanted to see the amphitheatre. I like history better than the present. History, at least, lets you choose your perspective.

When we were a little beyond the crest of the wheel it stopped with a jerk that pushed me forward in my seat, my stomach against the iron bar that held us in. I gasped and felt my face go cold, a darkness around the edge of my vision. Of course I didn't like heights. Bart hadn't been this tall. I shut my eyes and held the bar and the cold metal quickly grew hot under my palms.

'Are you all right?' Freya said.

I nodded, and opened my eyes slowly. We were rocking in the soft, hot air. Freya put her arm around my shoulder and I leaned against her. I realized I couldn't remember the last time we had touched. She wasn't a hugger. She had boyfriends – of course she did, quarterbacks, Phi Beta Kappas, captains of industry – but I had never quite been able to imagine what she did with them. Maybe just this. Her fingers squeezed the flesh of my arm. She nodded with her chin towards the amphitheatre.

'Do you want to go?'

'I don't know,' I said. I leaned back, felt better. 'Too many people. Look at the way they're all in lines. I bet they take you round in a group.'

'Yes,' she said. 'You're probably right.' We swung, and said nothing for a minute. 'Still.'

'I'll bet it's beautiful at night,' I said. Which at the time was not a comment I reflected much upon, or considered, or thought of as a challenge. Isn't anything beautiful at night? What isn't lovely when you can't really see it?

But that night, when we lay unsleeping in our bed, Freya said to me: 'We could go back, you know.'

'Where?'

'To Arles.'

'Well, yes. We could.' We had not really seen the place. We had spent too long at the fair. We had bought cotton candy and sugared nuts, and Freya, revealing a talent I had been unaware of, had shot at a lot of things, toy rifle clamped against her shoulder, one eye shut, her mouth set in a serious line that had made my own mouth smile. A row of cockeyed stuffed animals sprawled drunkenly on the desk on the far side of the room.

'No – I mean, we could go back now. Like you said. To the amphitheatre. At night. I'm not tired. Are you?'

'No,' I said. 'Not really.'

We lay on our sides, looking at each other. Or at least, she looked at me: I could feel the moonlight on my face and in my eyes, but her face, with her back to the open window, was obscured in shadow. I could see the shape of her cheek, her slightly open mouth, but her eyes were dark, deep in their sockets. There was no sound but the wind, and then a cat, somewhere, squealing as if it had been punctured, scrabbling on the pavement below.

My hand reached out, rested on her shoulder. My hand reached out – as if it had its own will. You don't believe these things until they happen. She had held my shoulder on the Ferris wheel, I held her shoulder now, my palm on the warm square of skin between her T-shirt and the sheet. What I wanted had no name, but the hole inside me filled and filled.

Freya sat up, swung her legs over the bed, sat up. Now the light would be on her face but her face was turned from me. I lay still. I felt cold. It was as if something had happened that I couldn't quite remember, or as if I had just woken up. 'Let's go,' she said.

And so we did. There was no one on the roads, and no one, when we got there, in the town, or so it seemed. Like there was a curfew, like there had been a plague. It was eerie. I didn't like it. We had driven all the way in a silence which seemed to me not our usual one – but then I thought, it's two in the morning. You're tired. This is stupid. You miss Bart. Did I? Or did I hardly remember him at all? I pressed myself back into the seat of the rented car and waited to see what would happen next, as if it were about to happen to someone else. Freya parked the car on some gravel by the amphitheatre, not a parking place, just a stretch of flat ground, but who would care at this hour?

We got out of the car into a stillness that was unlike any other city silence I'd ever heard: if I closed my eyes we could have been standing in the woods. The locking car doors clanked and echoed against the curved stone wall of the amphitheatre, rising high above us like a face turned sullenly away.

I followed Freya as she walked towards it. The wall was broken by gaping arches, one every twenty feet or so, and we went up to the one closest to us. An iron gate was stretched across its width, one of those collapsible ones like they have on old elevator doors, only this had no handle: only a padlock at its edge, and a small white sign tied with string to a central bar. *Fermé*, it said.

'What are we doing?' I said at last. I whispered, without meaning to. 'It's shut, we can't get in. We should have known it would be like this.'

'Look,' Freya said. She walked over to the edge of the gate and pulled it away from the wall. It was attached with chains whose ends had been bolted into the rock: when she yanked there was a gap of more than a foot. She slipped in, drawing in her hips, curving her back, pressing herself against the wall. And then she was inside. She grinned. The moon shone on her teeth. Behind her was a blackness that looked as solid as the framing stone. 'Come on,' she said. 'Let's get to the top.'

I thought you didn't like heights. No, that was just Bart. Her red tail-light always just ahead of me, pedalling up to the top of the hill. She must have known I was afraid. It must have been clear on my face. I suppose she thought I was afraid of the big

147

dark amphitheatre, its pitchy passages and worn-smooth steps; of the illegality of our escapade. And I was – I don't like heights, I don't like pranks, I don't like seeing what I can get away with. But that wasn't it. I was afraid too of the woman on the other side of the bars, who suddenly might have been anybody, whose years and years of silence suddenly echoed like the stone around us. There is the silence of ignorance and the silence of knowledge, and with a smile they can both look the same. I wondered if I had been missing something all along. But now it was too late for words. I nodded at her, and slipped round the gate.

The place was black like a cave. The moonlight entered only so far into the arch, and then ended in a neat white line on the sandy floor. We moved slowly: Freya, I think, had one hand on the inside wall, tracing its contour to find another opening, a stairway to take us up. I could tell she had found what she was looking for when she stopped and kicked at something: stairs. She must have leaned forward then because her words were distant and hollow: 'I think it gets lighter higher up. Just follow me. It's OK.'

It wasn't OK, but I followed anyway, like always. She went on, she led me up, up slippery dry stone steps whose centres had been worn to treacherous puddle shapes by centuries of climbers. We went higher and higher, up towards the light that I could begin to see peeking through chinks in the stone: cold comfort. I couldn't remember why we were here. I lived from stair to stair, and in imagining the climb down.

But it was beautiful at the top. The last flight of stairs rose up towards a square of night sky, and when we climbed out into it the amphitheatre dropped in silent tiers beneath us, the shadows cast by moon and stone so clean-drawn as to make the whole look two-dimensional, like a woodcut. All around it the city lay, blue as a Picasso, the river running flat and silver at its edge. The fairground seemed a thing abandoned, the Ferris wheel rising like a skeleton of itself into the sky.

The breeze turned. Freya had washed her hair with the lavender shampoo in our hotel bathroom.

'You were right,' she said. 'It's beautiful.'

'It is,' I said. We did not look at each other, but out at the carpet of roofs and shining water.

Where we were standing was flat: but a yard away the stone rose like a small hill, the top surface of an arch beneath. I could see it was like that all the way around. Freya began to walk and I followed, just a little way, climbing up on my toes to the crest of the first arch. Freya continued on down: she put out her hand to help me. I shook my head, stopped.

'I'm going to go around,' she said. 'You don't want to come?'

'No,' I said. 'I'm tired.' I wasn't, not anymore, but it seemed the easiest thing to say.

'Okay.' I watched her start off, rising up and over the little hillocks of the arches, walking along the flat with her long stride, and then, occasionally, leaping: which puzzled me at first, until I stood up on my toes and peered hard at the stone surface, and I could then see that every so often it was pierced by gaps, smaller than the stairway entrance through which we had emerged, but big enough to make Freya stretch to cross them. She would land with her back bent, stumbling forward with momentum.

I could see she wasn't afraid. I would have been afraid. Ever since the accident with the bicycle, I haven't cared much about physical courage. I've felt it was a virtue more to be deplored than envied. I thought of it as foolhardiness: of my own reticence as good sense. But now I was jealous. Jealous, and then angry, remembering the fall from my bike, my broken wrist, the spilling sky, the fear that never left me, the wanting that had been so hard to name.

I wish you were dead, I said. I think I said it aloud. And then she slipped.

'You saw her?' Renault asked. By then it was nearly five and he had finished his pack of cigarettes.

'Yes,' I said. 'I did.' I wondered if I should say I was sorry, or that I was sad, or that I didn't know what to do now, but he had asked a simple question and I thought I should just answer it.

'All right, Mizz Jenson,' he said. He sighed. It surprised me. He took a form from a drawer in his desk and began to write on it. He wrote for a long while, without speaking, and I just sat there, with nothing to do but watch his brown-stained fingers, his fountain pen, his eyes turned down to the page, hidden under their heavy lids.

Pyramid

On a moonless night the Pyramid hides behind a wall of onyx. The desert night drops down like a hawk and swallows the city, the river, the sea of sand all around and makes them as if they never were. Even in the palace the islands of light are few, and in between them the corridors open up to the thick blackness without walls or floors or windows. It's all the same, cavelike. Some people say you can vanish altogether on these nights: your hand disappears in front of your face and you go mad with imagining its outline, and by the time the light comes you are gone and no one can find you. My nurse used to tell me this to make me go to sleep, to stop me climbing into the seat by my window and watching the shimmering black. On these nights with no moon the light from the stars stops far short of the ground and hangs like a distant celebration at which no one is welcome, at which even the daughters of kings are not welcome. My father is the King. But the night hides nothing; not anymore.

★

At dusk the Great Pyramid begins to lose its shape. In the red light the edges of the stone seem to bleed out into the sand so that the two become one: a huge square-shouldered dune in the dying light. The sand laps against the base of the stone like the river laps against the bank, eating away at it, rubbing the corners smooth. There was gossip among the masons that the base would be quite worn down before the top was even begun. They had time to gossip, as they stood by the quay waiting for the barges of stone to arrive – and they came less and less often, as everyone knew. Everyone in the palace, and in the city too, I am sure: for the city is nothing now but a great machine to grind out men for the use of the King. If a family has two sons, one will go to work on the Pyramid: if three, two must be sent to haul stone. He who fathers four sons will send two to build, and one to serve in the garrison when he comes of age. This is the law. It is read out in the public squares by the crier who blows on his trumpet and calls, The Pharaoh is merciful and kind: the Son of the Sun spares each family a boy to till the fields: the people will never be hungry. The Pharaoh is merciful and kind: the Son of the Sun builds his monument to his glory which is the glory of the kingdoms over which he rules: from the tomb his perfected spirit will protect and bless his people, who send their sons to build in his name. The Pharaoh blesses his people while yet he lives: the Pharaoh blesses his people in the glory of his death.

I could hear it from my window. But I thought the people must be hungry: in the Palace there was much spice but little meat, and what there was had maggots beyond spicing. The

grain had the smell of cellars about it. I grew thin. If I lay on
my back I could feel the hollow in my belly, and cup my hands
around the hummocks of bone that rose at the level of my hips.
Not that I've ever been much bigger. My nurse used to say I
was scrawny, and make me drink the fatty cream that swirled
on top of the milk. I would never find a husband, she would
say, and we would laugh. I am betrothed to my cousin, my
father's sister's son. We played together as children, but now I
do not see him much. When I asked my nurse why she
shrugged and said, soon you will be weary enough of the sight
of his face.

Since I was born, the river has risen sixteen times. And sixteen
times it has risen since the King my father decreed that his
Pyramid should be begun. We have grown together. Because
the Pyramid was always there, it was easy not to notice it. I
never thought of it, any more than I would think of the nose
on my face when I looked in my silver mirror.

Of course, I heard it discussed. If I sat with my father I
would hear extravagant compliments made to it, comparisons
drawn, and would see the King's fine mouth turned in smiling,
his white teeth bared as he spoke delightedly of this weight of
stone, of that number of men, of his Chief Mason, born in the
slums of Cairo but whom the Pharaoh loved as his son. All this
I heard; and all this I ignored, as I sat on an ebony stool at my
father's feet with my hands in my lap, twisting the scarab on my
finger. It was hard to recall, with his eyes so dark and alive, that

my father was speaking of his death. Then he would be King forever. This was what he wanted most. It was the mason who could grant him his wish.

The Pyramid kept to itself. It grew out in the desert where it was necessary to peer hard to see its white surface swarming with men so that it seemed to be covered with a veil that rippled in the hot breeze. I looked at it very rarely. It is such a vast thing, its growth so slow – like the growth of a child – that daily observance is not rewarding. Once a year, maybe less, maybe more, I might look out and think, it has grown by the length of the last joint of my finger (my hand held out to the horizon, one eye shut against the sun). Don't stare out at the sand, said my nurse. You'll get a squint.

And so I would listen to her, and look away. Night would come, and seal the desert up, releasing only the clatter of the kites as they fought over something discarded. I hear they do not bury the bodies of the labourers who fall in the service of the tomb, that the sun and the kites take them quickly enough. The sand must be scattered with bones, sown lightly into the ground like seeds strewn on a field. When did I first think such a thing? Not so long ago. I can't remember, exactly. But I began to have nightmares, and my father's tomb began to be something no longer quite forgotten; a whisper in my ear or a footstep too close in the dark.

Not long after my dreaming began, the cargoes of stone stopped altogether.

★

Late one night, the Pharaoh came to see me. He drew the curtain of my chamber and stood in the little light that flickered out from a brazier by the door. My nurse, who was seated by my bed, dropped to her knees and put her face to the ground in front of the god.

I was not quite asleep. I opened my eyes, and did not move.

The Pharaoh put out his hand to my nurse, for she is not young, to lift her up. In these small ways my father is a simple man: he will do the necessary thing.

'You will leave us,' he said to her, and she nodded, and went towards her chamber, which is through a little door by the foot of my bed. The King held up his arm to block her passage, and she looked up into his face, so startled was she. 'Leave us alone,' he said. And so she backed out of the chamber and into the dark hall. I heard her steps for a long time. I often wonder, now, if she knew he would come. I used to think she knew all such things.

When she had gone, he came and sat on the edge of my bed, a thing he had never done before. One leg he drew in close to his body, and the other he stretched out on the floor; his sandal slid off and he flexed his bare foot. I sat up. I was glad to see him.

'My lord,' I said.

He said nothing, but lifted his hand to touch my hair, and looked down at me, and in his face was something I had never seen, a private face not exposed to ministers and servants, and kept well away from the sculptors who make him impassive and beautiful. The skin beneath his eyes looked fragile, and

155

below the lashes of one I could see a little blue vein that beat fast, like the heart of a bird. His linen shirt was not clean. For a moment I almost wondered if I was myself, if he was the Pharaoh, or if we had been shifted into some other life where we might sit like this together as if it were our custom. But it was not so.

He opened his mouth as if to speak, but made no sound, and shut it. One hand he kept on my head, in my hair, pulling it through his fingers, through his fist, and the other hand lay like a dead thing in his lap, weighted with gold. His eyes looked into mine, but the oil lamp cast a sheen across their surface through which I could not see. Then he twisted his neck, looked away, out the window to the desert, where the Pyramid breathed the day's heat back out into the night.

When he turned and stood, I saw his statue-face, the god's face, and I bent my head against its stare. I did not see his hand reach down to grasp the corner of the sheet that covered me, but felt the air cool on my body as he drew it quickly down to the foot of the bed.

I was naked, except for the knotted necklace that was once my mother's. I lifted a hand to cover myself, but the king took my wrist in his grasp to stop me. I closed my eyes, and heard his breath. When he spoke he was smiling; it was in the slant of his voice.

'The Pharaoh's daughter is beautiful,' he said.

I opened my eyes. And saw his face change again, felt him draw up the sheet fast to my neck and put his hand on my mouth to stop what words might come, but there were none to

be stopped. He kissed my forehead, and then rose and turned
his back and left.

Nothing was different; and nothing was the same. When my
nurse returned, I lay still as if I were asleep, but through half-
closed eyes could see the light of the waxing moon, and the
shadow of the Pyramid stretched across the sand.

Three days after the King's night visit, I returned to my chamber to find, not my nurse; another woman, younger, with a
proud neck and many jewels. I said to her, 'Where is my nurse?
I want my nurse here' – and I stood very straight because I am
the daughter of the King and she was to me nothing. But she
looked at me with black eyes that saw no princess, and she
laughed. She stepped forward, so that the little bells on her
ankles chimed, and she said, I am your nurse now. And she
kissed me. But her eyes never left my face, and my heart went
hard inside my chest. We said nothing else: she undressed me,
and sat at my side, and again I lay and did not sleep.

Or thought I did not: but in the morning I was awakened by
her ringing feet. She laughed again when she saw my open
eyes, and I wondered that she always laughed.

'My princess!' she said, and clapped her hands together. I sat
up, and she ran to me, carrying in her arms a dress of rich silk
dyed indigo, which she lay against my shoulder. It was soft as
fur, like nothing I had ever worn.

'Do you like it?' she asked eagerly, her voice low as if we
were playing a game together. 'It is beautiful, isn't it?' She

touched my face, my shoulder, with the back of her hand, her rings cool against my skin.

'Is it mine?' I asked, and she nodded as if just that thought made her happier than she could bear, and pulled me up with both of her pretty hands to dress me in it and brush my hair. It was a complicated shift of pleats and folds, and as she moved me this way and that her look was the look of the Pharaoh, as he'd stood that night by the foot of my bed.

The mason's name is Selket. He saw me in the indigo dress and he smiled, and touched the skin of my shoulder with his fingertips. When my pretty nurse said to me, Selket, the Chief Mason, is here to see the Princess, I did not know why. I imagined some matter of state. I imagined the Pharaoh was ill. I wondered why there was not some minister to see the Pharaoh's favourite. I wondered this until I felt the mason's calloused hands.

It was after noon when he arrived; the sun had not yet set when he left. Before he turned to go, he took from a pocket of his robe two little gold hoops set with turquoise beads, and when I would not take them from him, he set them on the table by the bed, and bent and kissed my cheek. He is not an unkind man. I know that now.

My nurse came and bathed me. I did not move: I let her lift my arms and pull the rings from my fingers as if I were to be laid out for embalming. Her face was smiling, as it ever was, but the smile was painted on like a mask, and she spoke very little. When I am with them, she sits behind a curtain and listens.

Before I went to bed that night, I spoke to her. She was standing by the window of her chamber, combing her thick hair, and she did not hear me come in. She must have thought I was asleep. Her face was clean of paint, and in the moonlight it looked almost plain.

'Do not tell me their names,' I said. 'Selket's name I know, and that is enough. Do not tell me anything about them.' I held out the little gold earrings the mason had given me, and she took them, and looked down at them as if she had never seen any such thing. 'There is only one thing I ask,' I said. 'Only one gift. Tell them that the Pharaoh's daughter has as her price what the Pharaoh so desires himself. I will accept nothing else.'

I left her standing with the jewels in her palm, and returned to my bed. Before the week was out, the Pyramid was darkened again with swarms of men, straining to draw the great stones up towards the sun.

It was Selket, of course, who first understood. Strange gifts came with stranger men: rich men bearing statues of Maat, with her feather of the soul, of Anubis and his scales, gifts of immortality. I made them take these away. Whatever I had become, I found that in the words of the Pharaoh's daughter there was still some power. But one afternoon Selket parted the curtain of my chamber, and sat down on my bed as the Pharaoh had. His face is made almost black from his years in the sun, his skin is creased and leathery. But the whites of his eyes are clear and bright, and when the dark pupils glitter like the eyes of a hawk, this means his smile will follow. He has more teeth than the usual.

One hand he took from behind his back and pulled me closer to him. Then he took my wrist and turned it, so my upraised palm was held out to him.

'I have brought you a gift,' he said.

'The earrings you gave me were very beautiful,' I said. 'My serving woman wears them. What have you brought me now?'

Boldness comes easily from my mouth now. Some other place inside of me has opened: it comes from there, like a second voice.

'I have brought what I bring for the Pharaoh. What he buys with his most precious of jewels.'

Selket kissed the palm of my hand. He grows bald at the top of his head. Then he took from behind him a small block of stone, small enough for me to hold in one hand, neatly cut, with sharp, square corners.

Rumour takes word of Selket's gift and sets it loose like a bird about the city. So now my little pyramid rises, a doll's grave, like its great father out in the sand. With each gift of stone it grows, the blocks so prettily and carefully cut that I wonder if it is not the Chief Mason himself who carves them.

But Selket I no longer see. Perhaps he is no longer the favourite of the King. It does not matter. Only the Pyramid matters: a living thing in the desert, a twin I never knew I had. No one, I think, will build my tomb. Tell them this: that when I die, I would not have my body dried and bound, but taken out to the desert, to the foot of my father's mountain. Leave me to lie where I belong, among the bodies of the men who built it, whose bones rattle in the hot wind.

A Few Hours at Home

He rang the first evening because he said he would; and whatever he said, he did, he was that kind of man. She could hear he
was in a callbox because of the undersea sound and the shrieks
of children zooming around her ear like flies.

'How is it?'

'It's all right. It's wet. Salim forgot his medication.'

He only had ten pence. His voice at the other end of the
phone was something she hardly noticed anymore, not like
before when it seemed like a stranger's. She had packed his
clothes for him.

'Do you have everything you need?'

'I think so. Shall I call tomorrow night?'

'Only if you have time,' she said. 'Don't worry.'

'I won't.' And he told her he loved her, and she said she
loved him too, which she did, she really did, and then they
hung up. He hung up first and just for a second she could hear
other voices on the line: other people's lives.

★

163

She made too much dinner because he was not there. It was remarkable what you could get used to, so fast. She put cold spaghetti and sauce into a plastic container and tidied it into the fridge, she did the washing-up, and in the kitchen she listened to the friendly television. She could hear people laughing but could not see what they were laughing about. She made a cup of tea and sat in front of the screen, letting it warm her.

It was eight o'clock. She would be asleep by eleven. He would be gone a week. She had not been without him before. Since she had been with him, that is. Which was not very long; she counted on her fingers: ten months. She did this counting more often than she realized. The solidity of the numbers it produced reassured her, as if they were proof of her own existence.

The week before they were married, she had gone into a barber shop and sat down in one of the shiny, leatherette chairs, waiting her turn. No one else was waiting, three men sat in the high, old-fashioned barber chairs with sheets wrapped tight around their necks. Sounds of scraping metal, like knives being sharpened, and the hum of clippers. She picked up a ragged magazine from the table in front of her and put it down again: Men Only, it said. Three pairs of eyes did and did not glance at her out of their disembodied heads, but the barbers did not look, only trimmmed and snipped, bending the compliant heads this way and that.

One of the barbers, the old one, agreed to cut her hair for her. She left with it in a plastic bag and walked home, letting the air ride over her scalp.

He had not said anything. He ran his hands over the velvet of her head and kissed her.

She liked to be exposed with him. He had split her open. When she was eleven she had had appendicitis: the surgeon had told her mother he had lifted her intestines out of her body and washed them. It was like that. Sometimes he shouted: he was jealous. Her old boyfriends hung in the air like ghosts.

But you have to trust me, she said.

I know.

Blue eyes, a broad strong face like a stone angel.

I trust you.

And he did.

When she turned off the television the house seemed very quiet, despite the grumbling of the street outside and the heavy tread of the Australians upstairs. She thought she might read, but her eyes were tired and hot from reading all day, burrowing into other people's lives on commission under the cool blue dome of the British Library. The British Library made her curious. The earnest silent people with their collections of tomes – *The Diaries of Joseph Banks* – an early collection of Browning – someone's desk piled with small brown volumes spattered with the carcasses of ancient insects and lettered in what looked like Icelandic. None of her business. Her business was not her business. All day she read and condensed, not absorbing information, letting it pass through her like water. She thought she was switched off: sometimes she could work for hours and not see the change in the slant of the light. But restlessness prickled under her skin. Without him here to distract her, it enveloped her like a scratchy blanket.

The telephone rang. When she answered it, there was silence, like breathing, and then the click of disconnection.

A number was taped to the handset: his number at the outdoor centre in Wales. She would not call it. Someone else would answer the phone, and fetch him. She had nothing in particular to say. He might worry. She sat down on the bed.

The telephone rang again. A while later. Ten minutes? She had just been sitting on the bed, staring at the curtains.

Hello?

Good evening, is Miss Solomon there?

There's no one here by that name, she said.

Is this – the voice at the other end, a woman, said her number.

Yes.

Then I wonder if I might interest you in our new line of Venetian blinds.

No thank you, she said, and hung up the phone.

It was nearly dark now. Her address book was squatting on the dresser like a shadow. She picked it up and leafed through the pages at the back, peering at her careful pencilling in the half-light. Names whose meanings had changed, some of them. Some of them – this aunt, that cousin – the same as ever, but others like ghosts, pieces of the jigsaw puzzle she had been, knots in which she had become entangled. Different houses, different streets, a memory of leaving over and over again in the bleak light of too-early morning, shivering from too little sleep.

She had always been glad to leave. But she had gone back, over and over again.

Until she had stopped. She was much happier now. She pushed her fingers up through the short hairs at the nape of her neck.

The address book hummed in her lap. She didn't want anything to be different. That is important to understand. But she saw that her happiness was a terrible, fragile thing, a blown-glass globe with her inside: at any time she could strike through the pane and everything would fall to bits. She could do it. It would be easy. All she had to do was dial a number.

She didn't want to, she didn't want to dial any numbers at all. She only wanted to sit, just now, in the darkness, knowing he was very far away ('Izetta, stop shouting! Sit down! Akbar, come back!'), wondering if he would imagine her sitting by the phone with a sledgehammer across her knees.

She had never tried to lie to him. She had never needed to. She didn't think she could. But people lied to each other all the time. She had lied to other people, though she hadn't enjoyed it, and had never thought it suited her. She had an honest face.

Where are you going?

Out.

Where, out?

Nowhere special. I'll be back soon.

She could look exactly the same. She could say the things she said to him every day, she could make his dinner and lie in their bed and put her mouth against his skin. But she could have secrets. There were people who lived their lives with secrets, who expected to have them, who didn't think that having secrets was unusual at all: they carried them around like change in their pockets. This one – the page in her address book where his name was written was worn thin, he had moved so many times – he had secrets. Once upon a time, she thought he didn't, not from her, but she had been mistaken. She hadn't called him for a while after that. Now, she never called him at all.

But she could. It was like standing in a Tube station and not jumping out in front of the oncoming train. The simplicity of the irrevocable amazed her.

It was dark now, black dark with an edge of city orange. The black pressed itself against the window as if it were trying to get in; it hissed under the ill-fitting glass like steam. She closed the book in her lap, clipped it shut, and put it back by the telephone. She closed the curtains, and got undressed.

The sheets were clean, and cold, and the room seemed very large without him in it.

She wasn't even tempted.

She wasn't. Only.

The phone rang five times before she picked it up.

Hello?

She was standing naked. A breeze moved against her skin.

It's me, he said. They're all in bed. I just called to say good-night. It's very beautiful here. The valley is very green. I wish you could see it.

We'll go sometime, she said. I miss you.

Me too. Did anyone call?

No, she said. People selling Venetian blinds. No one else.

The Bends

I press my foot hard on the gas and turn the radio down. Songs are like smells, insidious: they bubble into your blood and stay there like pearls of nitrogen, giving you the bends. They never go away, the bends: they cripple you for life. I turn down the radio because the song the station is playing is no good to me, not anything I can stand to hear.

The last time I'd heard it I was playing it myself, in my Walkman, running along the road to Grantchester. I ran every day then, the same route, from my house along the road past the Unicorn, the Green Man, the Red Lion, the Blue Ball. The seasons changed and I didn't notice. I ran along to the rhythm in my head and saw nothing.

So I don't know why I finally registered the white pick-up on that January day. I'd been running around it for weeks without seeing it, but that day I heard Mark's whistle, sharp and fluting and clear as a bird's. If birds whistle Sinatra. Anyway, there it was on the back of the truck, in sober Times Roman: M. J. Ashby, Master Thatchers in Reed and Straw. When I glanced up, he was perched on the roof of this overgrown doll's house with an armful of straw and the prettiest face I'd ever seen. I smiled at him, and waved as I passed. You have to understand I saw him as an abstract. What ran by that house was a woman deeply in love, in love with a tall doctoral student with a crooked smile and sea-blue eyes set wide apart like gems in an antique ring. I waved at the thatcher, the thatcher waved back. Once upon a time. The end. Except it wasn't; the end, I mean.

Two weeks later I was standing on a ladder angled unsurely on a scaffold, in a driving rain and freezing wind, soaked through and deliriously happy. I wasn't wearing gloves, and the aluminium ladder was so cold I was afraid my hands would stick to it as I clung to the sidebars. I was afraid the wind would blow me off: Mark had said this was possible. I was standing a few rungs below him, watching him work, my head about level with his hips. 'If your hands get too cold you can hold on to my legs,' he said, and I did. They were warm and solid, and I could feel the muscles shift slightly as his upper body twisted to work the straw beside him. The rain slid into my eyes, and I hid my camera underneath my coat. The rain ran off the peak of Mark's cap and on to the point of his nose.

The truth about my job is that most people, despite what they say, love to see themselves in black and white. After a few days of running by the house and actually seeing what was going on, I thought, there's something in this, so I asked if I could watch and take some pictures. Certainly, Mark said. And so began the passion I conceived for straw and the art of it, watching fascinated as Mark wove his roof so that the wild shafts became straight, ordered, secure, so that the strongest winds could not wrench them from their moorings though they were held only with pins of white hazelwood. I had thought I would spend a couple of days a week with Mark, take pictures, watch from the ground, stay out of the way. But before I knew it, I had reorganized my life so that every day, from eight until dusk, I was there with my notebook and camera.

But my notebook and camera gathered the golden dust that blew from the straw as Mark set me to work. He taught me how to bundle the straw, straighten it, clip the ends neat to ready it for the roof. I bundled and clipped until I was sweating in the cold wind and my back and shoulders ached. When the straw is tied, it must be dropped down hard on to a flat stone so that all the butts come even: when they do, the fat bundle rings like a bell. It was the most satisfying sound I had ever heard.

And so I resolved to be fearless. I have never been particularly afraid of heights, but the scaffold without a safety rail, the ladder balanced on only one of its legs: I wasn't comfortable in this place, at first. My feet suddenly felt separated from me by a great distance, and the space in between was awkward and unstable. But Mark watched my careful steps and concerted face and drew me gradually on, so that I hardly felt my fear slipping from me. Every day he would set me a task which now, looking back, I see was something that would stretch me further, take me one step higher, up towards the ridge of the house.

'Will you do me a favour?' Mark asked one day. Three weeks had passed; the new thatch nearly obscured the old. He didn't look at me, but kept on bashing at a hazel spar.

'What is it?' I was tentative, at this height.

'See those straws straggling up from the other side of the roof?'

I did. They were like whiskers pricking up from the front of the house, every which way.

'Got to get rid of them before we do the ridge. Take the shears, and clip them off.'

The way he spoke, it was understood that I would just do what he asked, that I would never say, I can't, I'm afraid. So the fear never took hold. I climbed down the ladder and collected the shears with their smooth wooden handles and curving, sinuous blades kept so sharp that when I touched them I could feel the wind blow through the hairs at the back of my neck. I had to climb one-handed, and finally stood almost at the top of the ladder, my left foot on the third rung down, my right on the very top rung. Tension made a girdle of taut muscle around my waist. Reaching up to the vagrant straws, I couldn't make the shears cut them. Mark watched, impassive.

'You're at the wrong angle,' he said at last. 'You've got to get higher, come at it from above.'

I permitted myself a laugh. 'Higher?'

'Get your left foot on the top rung of the ladder, and then

your other knee on the fixings above. Then you should be all right.'

I laid the shears on the sloping surface and climbed as he told me. My legs were tight as whipcord, twitching and flexing to balance, my toes curled in my boots. It was a stretch to get my knee on to the top spars, but finally I was there, hands free, leaning into the comforting coat of the roof beneath me. I reached for the shears and, pointing them at the ground below, found the straw cut quite easily. From here I could see down on to the other side of the house, the delicate pattern of spars that Mark had laid on the tops of the windows there, the sturdy pinnacles he had built and capped with crosses to keep the witches away. In the hazy distance, King's College Chapel was shell white, quartz seen through water, and the swallows, just returned from their winter in the veldt, dipped and wheeled around us. Sunny days had been rare, but at this moment I could barely recall the rain or the cold. At last, I turned to Mark who stood so easily against the ruddy bricks of the chimney. His eyes were deep in shadow, but I could see the spider-lines of his smile at their corners.

But the doctoral student, you ask, what does he make of all this? He is perplexed. He is, I think, bored. A curtain closes behind his blue eyes when I tell each day's tale, and my excitement is blunted, wearing against the armour of his puzzlement. So I become quiet, listen to his days and keep mine to myself. They are a secret then, and there is a new joy in that because now – you saw this coming, didn't you? – there is another secret too. I have fallen in love with the thatcher.

★

This road is too narrow for the traffic it carries. I am driving through Norfolk, and that in itself should set me off, though I am not well-enough acquainted with the wide, flat land to recall exactly where Mark and I drove one Sunday in February when we set off together to look at reed beds. He suggested the outing: he said he'd never actually seen water reed growing, and would like to. We should make a day of it. I was very casual. That would be nice, I said. We were standing in a sunny wood when he asked, a coppice where we had gone to cut hazel for spars. The fire he'd built spat and rang, and when I turned towards it I could no longer feel the heat of my face.

We set off with purpose; but although Mark drove the battered pick-up at a clip, our journey seemed aimless. He took me to the farm where he had worked before he had become a thatcher, showed me where he had lived, told me what the life was like. I sat silent as he shouted over the roar of the road. I wondered if I could fit myself into his story, his old knowledge of the land and its ways that separated us as if by centuries. Each tree, each bird, each hill meant something to him, and slowly, slowly began to mean something to me. The countryside poured around us, its hieroglyphs deciphered for me as we drove.

We never saw the reed beds. It began to rain, and off-duty, Mark was no more eager to get soaked than I was. But the day ate itself away, and it was nearly dark when we passed a field of sheep. The sky had turned a mottled grey, hanging low off the ground, and our headlights had begun to flicker on the wet tarmac ahead. We were stuck behind a tractor, and Mark was gazing out the side window.

'Hang on,' he said, and pulled the truck up sharply.

'What?'

'Can you see –' He was peering across me, leaning over my lap. He didn't smell of anything. This was the strangest thing about him: no matter how hard he worked, no matter how close I stood to him, I never smelled anything, not sweat, not soap, nothing. It was the same thing now. The nearness of his skin, the delicate line of his jaw and the pale flesh below his ear, the sight of these pressed the small of my back into the worn car seat and leaned a weight on my bones; but it was sight alone that crushed me. Mark pointed, twitched his chin towards the field. 'That sheep, all by itself – just a white shape – there –'

I peered into the gathering dusk, my hand out against the glare of the glass, until I saw what he saw, the lonely, still shape away from all the other shapes.

Mark clicked on the hazard lights and got out of the truck. I followed. We clambered up the slight bank at the side of the road, and Mark stepped carefully over the low wire fence. He held out his hands to me. 'Careful,' he said, 'it's electric.'

His were small hands, strong, permanently darkened by straw dust ingrained in the skin; but his palms were cool and supple. His skin on mine was a little shock, not so bad as the fence might be. I stepped up and over, and then there we were in the darkening field. He was smiling, a secret, foxy smile, and I could just see his crooked teeth, my heart high in my throat. I dropped my hands and shoved them back in my pockets. Mark strode off across the lumpy ground, and I followed half a pace behind.

'It's not running from us, you see,' he said. 'It's cast.'

'Cast?'

'When they have a lot of wool on them, sometimes they fall and can't get up. They'll lie there for days. They can die like that, if no one finds them.' He glanced around. 'I just hope some farmer doesn't think we're sheep-thieves. We don't want a shotgun pulled on us.'

The sheep was lying on its back, legs splayed like bent sticks, and it bleated as we approached. Its face was black and its wool was heavy and thick. Even I knew that sheep are never white, but this one seemed particularly dirty, with clods of earth matted into its coat. There was a pile of shit at its back end. Mark pointed to this. 'See? Been here a while already. Come on this side, with me.'

He squatted down by the sheep, at its tail, and I did the same up at the head. We slipped our hands beneath its greasy back, and Mark, bouncing a little on his haunches, breathed, 'one – two – three – ' and we pushed, heaving the startled animal over. It scrambled for a moment in the dirt, down on its knees, back legs buckling up, and then darted away, one hoof catching Mark a blow on the shin as it dashed to the crowd of its fellows huddled in the far corner of the field.

Mark exhaled sharply, and then fell. One fist dug into the earth and he toppled, looking, just for a second, like the sheep as it rose – but backwards. It happened too fast for me to do anything. I just stood there as he collapsed on to his back, clutching at his leg and groaning.

So I squatted down and slipped my hands underneath him.

'One – two – three –' I said, and then we both laughed loudly enough to make all the sheep stampede away toward the barns in the distant gloom. I held out my hands and he took them, pulling himself up and stumbling a little, lifting his weight off his injured leg.

'Am I completely filthy?' He was still laughing.

'I can't see,' I said, trying to brush him off, running my hands down his shoulders and back. 'No, it's no good. I can't see.'

He turned towards me then, and said my name, and I stepped into his clasp and that was all. It was easy. We stood, in a sheep field, just like that, with the sun gone down and the moon a thin crescent low in the sky. The dark smell of the earth rose off him like smoke.

The end never comes when you want it. I wanted to put it there, and leave you thinking of the two of us entwined under the arching sky. But it doesn't work that way. That embrace, that kiss: we were diving down too deep, too fast and I came up still holding the cool night air in my lungs, my breath explosive at the surface, the crippling gas already slicing through my veins. We were not suited to each other, I know. The tall doctoral student is forgiving, and gives me a ring with stones the colour of his eyes. I won't put it on yet: I am waiting for the dark ridges of callused skin that mar my hands to fade back into my flesh.

Back Home

I remember thinking that grey, hot afternoon would swallow me up. Or eat away at me, like acid: after so many years in Oregon I had forgotten about New York in summer. It caught up with me soon enough. The feeling I had on 57th Street was no different from the jawlocking tension I used to feel all the time when I lived here. It was why I left.

But you can never leave home, not really. I'd been trying since I was old enough to take a bus. Riding home from school I would pretend that I was someone else's child, at some other school, in some other city. But this time I wanted to be here. I'd bought the airline ticket and come home. I walked along Park Avenue with the keys to my mother's apartment in my purse.

480 Park Avenue is a grand, old-style New York apartment building, made from big strong blocks of yellow stone and fittings of iron and brass. You couldn't build something like that

now in the city, even if you had all the money in the world. It is what I have always known as a 'feet-first' building: the only way anyone leaves is feet first, in a box.

The doorman didn't recognize me. Why should he?

'I'm Mrs Sullivan's daughter,' I said. I took out the keys, two shiny Yale keys.

'Oh, yes of course. Go right on up. Eighth floor.' He smiled at me. He was an enormous black man and looked fantastical in his doorman's uniform, which was like a crazy morning suit, jet black wool with yards of dark gilt trim, frogging, I think it's called. But it was a costume well suited to the lobby of this place. I stopped at the head of the stairs and looked at it again.

I'd barely noticed it, growing up. Children aren't impressed by marble and velvet, but my mother was, and she was always pointing things out to me, not just here but all over the city, everywhere we went. I would stare resolutely downwards. Now I saw what she meant: this was a lobby for Vanderbilts, for Hearsts and Woolworths. A hundred yards long, black and white marble tiles covered with a strip of deep-red Persian carpet, all the way down. Ornate Louis-Something benches every few yards, rest for the weary. A procession of crystal chandeliers like frozen wedding cakes hung upside down, and enough brass to keep an army of ill-paid workers – 'little men,' my mother would call them, a 'little man' to restring her pearls, a 'little man' to clean the drapes – polishing for a week. It was like I'd never seen it before, and it was only now, now that she was gone, that I could begin to see what it meant to her. Her mother spoke only Gaelic to the day she died. After she married, my mother never spoke the language again.

I was nine years old. I was walking with my mother towards this same block, this same building, only we were coming from uptown, walking briskly through the Presbyterian wealth of Park Avenue. New York was very different when I was a little girl, it wasn't like it is today, but even then Park Avenue was something else altogether. The streets were sedate and quiet, almost like a library full of musty leather and gold leaf. No one moved too fast, no one ever ran; even the swift click, click, click of my mother's heels seemed excessive. But my mother never walked slowly, she never strolled. At the weekends, when the maid went home and she had to take me to the park, she was impatient, sitting on benches, crossing and recrossing her pretty legs while I chased squirrels. I never kept her too long. I could always see she was trying.

But now we were moving at her pace through the sharp November air, and I would sometimes trot to keep up. It was the afternoon. Why was I not in school? Why was she home from work? I don't remember that.

I remember, in order, three things: waiting at a light, hearing a siren, seeing my mother's chin flick up to follow the sound. You didn't hear a lot of sirens on Park Avenue. The police car yanked to a halt a couple of blocks away, and I could see that a small crowd had already gathered at the crosswalk where it had stopped. My mother craned her neck. The uptown light changed, but we didn't cross: holding my hand, my mother pulled me west, to cross Park, to the side of the street where the police car had stopped.

As we got closer to the small knot of people, my mother's head dodged back and forth as if trying to see around shoulders and through backs. I could see mostly legs. Finally, we were there, and instead of dashing past the crowd – 'Rubberneckers,' I had heard my mother say derisively, more than once – she began to push purposefully through, gripping my hand so tightly that my fingers squeezed against each other and her heavy rings dug into my bones. I had never seen my mother shove anyone before. People let her through. She said 'excuse me' and 'pardon me' so firmly I guess they thought she had a right to be there.

Now I remember: two policemen, one pacing back and forth, leaning into the car and shouting into his radio, pacing again. Another policeman, without his coat, his arms very white, kneeling by a shape on the ground. On the shape was his coat. Then I saw that the shape had legs, and then the winter sun caught the dark puddle in the gutter, and I saw that it was not melted snow, but blood. In the same instant, my mother leaned down to me and hissed, 'That's why you *never* cross the street without looking both ways.'

I suppose I screamed then, or cried, because the standing policeman dropped his radio and looked up, and ran at us, his gun and nightstick flapping on his thigh. He pushed my mother out of the way, turned me around, his big red hands on my shoulders, yelling something. We were sucked back out through the crowd, which was bigger now, and back out on to the stillness of Park Avenue.

My mother didn't pause for breath. She swept me along again, click, click, click, almost home. I guess she was embarrassed, having been shouted at by a policeman. She never said anything else to me about crossing streets, but then, she never had to.

The Yale keys stuck in the locks, and wouldn't turn. As if they hadn't been used in a long time, though I knew that wasn't the case. It just felt that way. I hadn't turned those keys – top to the left, bottom to the right – in years.

When the door at last swung open, the apartment puffed out a hot breath, a strange smell, not one I associated with my childhood or my home. I had prepared myself for a particular smell, of furniture polish, floor wax, all the little unnameable things I knew, as I came up in the elevator. It wasn't here. This smell said: disuse, neglect, sadness, age. I turned on the light.

Six of the nine bulbs in the chandelier weren't working. They were those little flame-shaped bulbs, not very bright in the first place, and the light they gave now was dim and sombre. I hurried in, not even putting down my bag, and threw on all the lights in the living-room. The shades were down; I suppose my mother's last maid must have done that when she died. I pulled them up. The natural light made things a little better, but not much.

Was it always like this? I remembered a vivid brightness,

despite the dark wooden Spanish floor and heavy antique furniture; but looking around I could see that it wasn't only the chandelier in the hall that was missing bulbs. Every sconce lamp along the walls was missing a bulb, sometimes both, like missing teeth. It made me angry, just at whom I wasn't sure. Or is that not true? It made me angry at the maid, Carla, she was called. Why hadn't she replaced the bulbs? Any idiot could put in a new bulb. Why was my mother living in this oppressive darkness?

But my mother, for the past two years, had hardly moved out of her bedroom. These lamps, carefully placed to show paintings and furniture, walls and floors, to the best advantage, didn't matter anymore. And I had been in Oregon. I had not once come back east. Poor Carla.

I went to leave my bag on the little marquetry table in the front hall, a pretty thing, like a delicate desk for a fine lady of two hundred years ago. My mother always told me, especially as she got older, how valuable it was. Her furniture was her passion; she bought most of it in Paris, just after the War, travelling into every far-flung *arrondissement* for a better deal. She was a real shark, my mother. It's turned out that most of the deals were on her. Several weeks ago an appraiser for Christie's looked over the apartment. She was right about the little desk: eighteenth-century, beautifully made, worth a lot of money. But everything else – the legs were Louis XVI, but the rest was not; this was a brilliant copy but the screws gave it away – Mr Dawson was very thorough. I was glad that my mother never heard what he had to say about her beloved 'pieces'; but somehow I couldn't quite believe that she didn't always know. You're an heiress, she had said. The furniture alone. But it wasn't true.

As I turned to go towards the bedroom, I saw myself in the mirror across the hall. A mirror in a frame, like a painting, an old mirror, of course, with those dark spots at the edges from flawed silvering. Not a mistake: before they knew better. And there I was, just the same as I was in Janet's bathroom that morning: my hair quite grey now, not 'salt and pepper', like I used to say, and my eyes beginning to go a bit yellowy in the whites, with fine lines stretched out from the corners. My skin darker, coarser, by no means young. Skin with knowledge, skin with experience, skin not the skin of a daughter anymore. Was I a daughter at all? I am an orphan, I thought, looking at that well-used face in the mirror, and laughed, because orphans are wide-eyed waifs in dresses a size too small. It has taken me this long to be an orphan, I thought: and I've grown out of it. I touched my face in the mirror, or where my face looked to be; two fingers almost met across half an inch of reflected space.

The mirror was grimy. It had the darkness not only of age but of dirt as well, a thin film of oily dust. I began to peer closely at the walls, the furniture: it was everywhere. Not on every surface, but pervasive, giving a dull sheen to the backs of chairs and the tops of tables. Cigarette smoke, cooking fumes, New York City airborne sludge – resting lightly here and there, perched on the edges of things like an uneasy guest. It was like the bulbs all over again: how could this be? I had known my mother to stand on a footstool and run a white-gloved finger over the top of a wardrobe door.

The kitchen was worse. It was unashamedly greasy, and clicking open cupboards I found ancient bags of flour hard as rocks, rice spilled and picked at by roaches and maybe even mice, and countless cans of ready-made food: corned-beef hash, chili, Spaghettios. For my mother? My mother, the chef, the despot of the kitchen? I was pushing through the cupboards, searching for some sign that things were the way I remembered them, but found nothing. I found her china cracked and dusty. I tried to recall if I had ever met Carla, so I could put a face to my anger, but nothing came, only a vague blue polyester dress and a white apron. Sensible shoes and an accent. It could have been anyone. And then, staring down at a can of peas, I suddenly thought: maybe my mother didn't care anymore.

We were standing at the window in my father's room, looking out. My father was holding my hand, which even then, at ten years old, I found extraordinary. My father held my hand in the street, to protect me, I suppose he thought, but inside – never. For a long time we stood in silence, just seeing what we could see, which wasn't much at all. The city seemed a random scattering of grey protuberances poking out of a vast field of white. It was six-thirty in the morning.

Later, my father told me that the blizzard of '47 was as bad as the one in '88, when he was a little boy. I had never seen anything like this. The radio was grumbling in the bathroom, and the announcer was saying twenty-three inches of snow, maybe more. I knew there would be no school; I knew my father had no hope of getting down to Wall Street, where he worked. It seemed like the end of the world. Life was very regular for me then, despite the endless chain of different nannies and maids to meet me after school. We had the same thing for dinner on the same day of each week, I had oatmeal for breakfast every morning and the clothes I would wear each day were laid out for me when I woke up. I had no initiative for irregularity. I looked up at my father, his bald head and already old face, and wondered. He looked down at me and smiled, and then, still holding my hand, led me into the kitchen to make me breakfast.

Again, there is a gap of memory. I wish there wasn't; because what I next recall seems so strange to me that I want to know how it came about, and can't imagine the conversations that led to it, the steps that led me and my father and my mother, all swaddled in layers of clothes and stout, wool-lined galoshes, out into the still air at eight o'clock in the morning. I am sure my mother wanted to stay inside: how did my father – or I – persuade her to come out? What I do remember is that as we stepped out on to the small patch of clear sidewalk beneath the awning of our building, I thought: this is like a family. This is what real families do. And I remember being surprised, because weren't we a real family anyway?

Of course we weren't. I know that now. My mother worked – not as a secretary or anything, but in an important job on Seventh Avenue – when no one else's mother did. People thought there was something wrong with her. People thought my parents must be getting divorced: and no one did that, either. Or at least, they didn't talk about it, and being a child of divorced parents was almost as bad as being an orphan, or having an incurable disease. People talked about my parents. I knew that, and I knew that they had terrible fights, late at night, when I was meant to be asleep, and I was sure that quiet Mrs Baker didn't fight with Mr Baker that way, or Mrs Stern with Mr Stern. They were regular mothers. Sometimes, lying in bed and hearing the muted howls in the kitchen, I would invent for myself a regular mother. She made cookies instead of soufflés, and she was at home when I got back from school. In the Oregon mountain stillness of three in the morning, when I find myself at my kitchen table with a cup of tea, that shadowy, flour-dusted woman still comes back to me.

Real families. We walked out into the snow, taking giant steps like the boy with the seven-league boots, sinking into the snow and laughing. I could barely push my way through – it came above my waist, in places – and at last my father put me on his shoulders.

For two hours we walked, heading downtown, meandering along as best we could on the route my father usually took to his office. He walked there, every day. The farther down we got the quieter the city seemed. It was as if all New York had woken, turned on their radios, looked out the window, and rolled over and gone back to sleep. We were the first ones to break the brilliant, opalescent crust of the snow, and we stumbled on, straying into the street because we couldn't see where the sidewalk ended, bumping into the cold lumps of cars that had been completely buried by the snow. I walked through drifts much taller than me, and looking up could see nothing but the black spines of streetlights and the office buildings with darkened windows, every ledge piled with white powder, making flickering patterns that rose up into the white sky.

My mother's nose was red and the hair that stuck out from beneath her woolly hat – not an elegant hat at all – was awry, like mine. She wound her arm around my father's waist and they were both so young, just then, in those few hours in the snow. I could hear our three breaths entwined: not just see the steam from our mouths but hear us breathing, it was that quiet. The snow baffled the echoes of our laughter, made them disappear, and let only the soft, delicate notes peal through: the clink of the top buckle on my coat, my mother's earrings ticking against her scarf.

At 23rd Street my father stopped, very suddenly, and stood still, holding up his hand: listen. My mother and I went quiet at once, and the three of us huddled together. For a moment I couldn't hear anything, and then, through the thin air, I heard the gentle ringing, jingling round the corner, a sound I knew even though I had never heard it before. Sleigh bells.

A man in a top hat and a big red scarf held the reins, which lay lightly on the back of a small, shaggy pony trotting quite easily through the snow, pulling a sleigh like the ones I'd always seen on Christmas cards, all curving lines and polished wood, riding on wide shiny skis. The pony's harness glittered silver in the bright light, for it was hung all over with bells that made the clearest, merriest sound I had ever heard. I remember my mouth fell open. It was so extraordinary: the magical, silent city, the long hilarious walk, and now this, slipping past us on 23rd Street, the solitary driver tipping his hat to us, the only other people alive in the world.

When he had gone, we walked for a while longer, until my mother began to get too cold. I think we took the subway home. That man must be dead now, like my parents, though the sleigh may still be around somewhere, and the harness with its silver bells.

After about an hour I couldn't bear the kitchen anymore, and stepped back from the mess I had made. It looked far worse than it did before. I had disembowelled it: decaying packets and dusty tins were scattered on all the surfaces, the silver, unpolished for years and bound in ancient plastic bags, lying among it. I'll have it all cleaned out, I thought; I can't even look at what there is to save or sell with all this mess. I would get some cleaning company to scour the place top to bottom. I would have nothing to do with it.

And so at last I wandered into my mother's bedroom. I did wander: I went slowly, via the living room, the fireplace, the sofa, touching the furniture and the pictures of myself as a little girl, always smiling, always pretty in the immaculate stylish clothing my mother made for me. What did she think, when I moved out of ballgowns and permanently into sneakers? She never said anything. I know what she thought.

The bedroom looked more like a hospital than anything

else. I was glad not to recognize it. Besides my mother's own pink-upholstered divan bed, there was a hospital bed; there were a couple of oxygen tanks, looking rusted and untrustworthy; there was a wheelchair. My mother's furniture – the bed, the pale, spindly-legged desk, the armoire – seemed to cower among all the shiny metal. The props that had supported my mother all her life had become, in her last hours, useless and archaic nuisances. Nurses and aides had tripped over them and cursed them, had worn down the carpet, had told hearty, healthy jokes in this cloistered and ladylike atmosphere. I thought, she must have wanted to die. And then I remembered: she did.

I stood at the threshold. When I was little, as a special treat my mother would let me go through her closets and drawers, try on her clothing and jewels, look at the dead faces of families gone by displayed in stiff matte photographs. Auntie Evelyn. Uncle Sean. Cousin Ira. The names meant nothing to me, and sometimes nothing to my mother: but then we were a family creative with its history. My mother was born Maire Sullibhean, New York Irish, a Westie. My father was Harry Friedman, from Chicago, a good Jew. They married in London, where they had met, and became Mr and Mrs Harry Sullivan. They were going to move to New York and my father thought he'd be better off without his Jewish name. My mother slid into being simply Mary. If they made themselves over – what does that make me?

The family photographs were in the top left-hand drawer of my mother's dresser. I pushed past the wheelchair and opened it – it still stuck – and there they were, the familiar non-existent faces that might as well have been bought in an antique store. But I remembered them. Even if those faces were false, even if someone, some Sullivan or Friedman along the line had acquired them, a long time ago I had called them my family, and my family they remained. I laid them out like cards on the dresser top, moving back the little footed teak boxes that held my mother's jewellry. Then I opened them: no one told me to put the pictures back first. I wanted to leave them out.

My mother favoured turquoise, turquoise and gold. She had opals too, and diamonds – my father had liked to give her diamonds – and it was all here in these boxes, jumbled up together like treasure in a pirate's chest. This was no sign of decay; it had always been like that. I remember sifting through the thin ropes of gold, letting odd loose pearls drift through my fingers as I looked for the pieces I liked, wanting to hold them next to my skin. I think my mother never got used to owning jewellry. She wore it beautifully, she could wear the most ornate pieces with bright ease, but secretly I think she was always surprised that she had any at all. So she squirrelled it into these boxes, making glittering little mounds of treasure. It hadn't been wise: stones had fallen out and slipped to the bottom of the heap; pearls needed restringing. I couldn't see myself doing any of it. I held a necklace against my throat: a wide band of deep turquoise beads, with a baroque back-fastening: a flower made from a large centre pearl and petals of opal and sapphire. She had adored this necklace, and I had too, as a child, and had dreamed of growing up and wearing it, of holding up a slim stem neck circled with gems. Now, I could not imagine being the person who would wear such a piece. I put it down on top of the photographs. Eyes and noses peeked out from between the stones.

I shifted my weight from my right foot to my left foot and opened the closet door. One hand still hovered by the jewellry boxes; but no, I would put it all away later. I felt a sense of urgency, as if someone were about to walk in on me – not my mother, just someone – and I felt furtive about what I was doing. But why had I come in the first place? Well, to clean things out, to tidy up. But that wasn't what I was doing at all. Whatever it was, I mustn't do it for long.

The closet looked slightly different, at first glance. There were clothes I hadn't seen, a walker, and a cane. But the yellow wallpaper was just the same, and up the jamb of the door were wiggly pencil marks with dates underneath them. The first one was three feet off the ground, the last, a few inches over five feet. My height. Both my father and mother were short. Height was important to them. In that regard, I was always a disappointment, although both of them, when I came home from a summer away, would greet me with: 'How tall you've grown!' – long after my growing days were over.

I knelt on the floor, and began to open little doors all around, closets within the closet. Shoes: some fashionable, some hardly worn. A pair of hideous laced 'orthopaedic' shoes my mother had acquired when she had been plagued by bunions some years ago. I don't think she ever brought herself to wear them. An antique sewing-machine: antique only by accident, for it had been the one on my mother's table all the years I was growing up. Now it was old and cumbersome, ridiculous almost with its black enamel and chipped gold leaf. Singer. Stray belts, odd buckles, candlesticks, a footstool, all the haphazard stuff of a lifetime, all the things I know she swore to organize next week, next month, next year – don't I do the same? Strange to think that there comes a point when there is no more *next* – I wonder if she thought of all these things as she lay in that high metallic bed, no longer able to sort and discard and give things to the Catholic Home for the Aged.

I kept pulling things out to get at them, to see better, and they began to heap up in a pile around me. I began to tire. My knees started to ache the way they do so often now – and I was just about to get up when I reached far back into one of the small dark cupboards and pulled out the last thing in it, a thick, leatherbound book, the binding of which was bent out of shape from all the papers that had been stuck into it, almost every leaf having another leaf inserted by it. I opened it: it was in Hebrew. A Torah. But there was no name in it, no dates: I thought it must have been my father's. Starting from the back – it seemed the logical thing to do – I pulled out one of the extra leaves. It was a folded sheet of thick blue paper, the good kind that has been made from cloth. It had an engraved letterhead, in dark green, almost black ink: Monmouth Haven School for Girls. The date was scrawled underneath by me in handwriting that has hardly changed in forty years – September 12th, 1951.

My first year at boarding school. I didn't read it; I didn't need to. I glanced at it and took in dozens of exclamation points and question marks, wild capital letters and the breathless air that pervaded the paper itself. I felt myself grow hot and red with embarrassment. I turned the pages of the Torah. All letters, all from me, not in any particular order, but surely every letter I ever wrote was saved here, in this old hidden book. My father's bible in my mother's closet: who was saving them? Did they do it together? I was quite amazed. It was an act of such clumsy tenderness – the ancient family book, the haphazard filing – performed by people unused to tenderness of any sort. Not that I felt unloved. Not exactly. But the difficult words were not in our vocabulary, and the images I hold are more of the strange and the painful than of the good and kind. Except for that morning in the snow, like an event out of someone else's life. I wished that there were, in these crumbling pages, a letter about that. There wouldn't be, of course: we were all together. But I remembered these letters, their brittle, gay tones squeezed out of my mother's eternal dictum: if you can't say anything nice about something, don't say anything at all. There was a lot I didn't say. I would have liked to think there was something real in here, but I was pretty sure there wasn't, and I couldn't bear to look.

I slid the little book back where I found it, and got up, my knees aching. My mother's things lay in piles at my feet; stepping back I looked at the scattered jewels, the photographs exposed to the light. The furniture pushed astray, the ransacked kitchen. My mother would barely have recognized the place. Doctors, nurses, helpers had all trooped through here, and now, at long last, I had come.

I had no business here. Like all the others – tearing apart the things my mother loved, the things I had no need for and had never wanted. So much of it I had already promised to give away. Why had I come here in the first place? Why didn't I leave it all to my cousin Claire? She lived in New Jersey, after all.

I wanted to go home to Oregon, to go straight from Park Avenue to the airport. I turned my back on my mother's plundered bedroom and started clicking off the lights I had turned on, pulling down the shades, closing the kitchen door so that I wouldn't have to see the mess again. I gathered my purse from the table and yanked open the front door, letting the yellow light of the hallway spill into the now darkened house.

Dark but for the light in my mother's bedroom, which I had forgotten to turn off. Conscientiously, I went back, trying not to look at the mess I had made. I pushed down the switch, and then, in the dim half-light of an old apartment with windows facing a side street, opened the closet door and retrieved the little book. It wouldn't fit in my purse, so I held it in my hand, and raised it high to hail the taxi that would lead me, eventually, back home.

Mysteries of the Ancients

'I am thinking,' my father says, his hands set like a little teepee under his chin, 'that it would be nice to build one of those in America.'

'One of what, Dad?' my brother asks. John is twelve. He doesn't have problems with questions like that. We are sitting in the living room, the three boys, Mom used to say, watching the TV with the lights off. Now that my mother's gone, Dad doesn't bother to tell us it's bad for your eyes to do that. The TV is a big blue eye in the centre of the room, and we are shadows in the flickering corners.

'Like Stonehenge,' and he nods towards the TV. We are watching a show that's on every week, *Mysteries of the Ancients*, and this week it's all about big stone things that no one seems to know much about.

'What?' my brother says. He rolls his eyes at me: I can see the whites turn in the light from the TV, like cat's eyes in the dark. Dad is not looking at either of us, but staring at the TV.

He's turned the sound down so it's only pictures, pictures of stones.

'You couldn't use stones,' he says, more to himself than to us. 'Stones are kind of bulky and anyway, there aren't any around here.' He stops, taps his fingers together, and then looks at me, smiling. 'And stones aren't very American, are they?' Does he want me to answer? But then he goes on. 'I'm sure,' he says, 'that there are other things you could use. All you'd have to do is give it a little careful thought.'

He turns back to the TV, puts the sound up again. Now they're showing someplace in Ireland, some big ugly tomb. The camera makes circles around it, and they play weird Irish music. My father points to the set.

'I've read about that one,' he says. 'There's a door to it, with a slit in it or something, and on just one day of the year, at just one time, the sun comes in and makes this bright light all inside the tomb.'

John, who has been asking to watch some sitcom, shrugs: 'So?'

Dad turns to him, really slowly, as if while he's moving he's thinking of important things, as if the way he's moving is making him think of important things.

'That's a good question, son.' I can't remember him ever calling either of us *son*. It's like something out of a book. 'That's a good question. I wonder that too. What's the big deal? But I'm looking at those pictures and I'm thinking that it is a big deal. It isn't about money. Anybody can have money. What it's about is energy.' He says that last word slowly, en-er-gy, and stops just before he says it, like he didn't know what it was going to be until the second it actually came out of his mouth. 'Energy. That's the important thing.' He curls his hands into fists and presses the knuckles together. 'That's what we need.'

He's staring at the TV and I can see he's thinking hard. Since Mom left he thinks all the time. Mostly it doesn't bother me. Dad is a man who can do anything, in his way; not that he's ever done anything *important* in his life, not in the way anybody looking from the outside would see it. But when he says that word, energy, there is something new in his voice. My father's a practical man, he flicks past Oral Roberts on Sunday mornings and says, 'You'd think Darwin would've taught them a lesson.' But he says that word like it is religion, like whatever it is, he's going to get us some.

My mother left us six months ago. I can't take this anymore, she said, I just can't take this. She was standing in the kitchen when she said it. I was sitting at the table at the time, trying to do my homework, and I looked up at her straight, thin back silhouetted against the window. Her hair was in a thick braid down her back, with little hairs standing out from it, wild, escaping the braid and the rubberband down by her waist. She turned towards me, and looked at me hard, as if I was someone she'd never seen before.

'I was your age when Matthew was born,' she said. Matthew is my brother that died when he was two. My older brother. I think he still is my older brother, even though we were never in the world at the same time. 'I was just like you, just the same.' I didn't really know what she meant. Her hands were on her hips, leaving wet marks on her pants. She sighed, and dropped her shoulders down like she was tired. 'I'm sorry, honey,' she said. 'I'm sorry.' And she kissed me on the forehead and walked out of the room.

I went right on doing my homework. I'd heard her say funny things before; my Dad said that's why he loved her, she was so unexpected about everything. I thought maybe she'd had a hard day at the plant where she worked, that she'd go out back and have a cigarette, come back and finish making supper. But she didn't.

At seven o'clock my Dad came into the kitchen. 'Hi, Champ,' he said to me, and put his hand on my head. 'Where's your mother?'

'I don't know,' I said. 'I thought she was out back. She seemed kind of fed up. She hasn't come back in here.'

She wasn't anywhere. She'd packed a suitcase and gone. That was it. Like she said, I guess she couldn't take it anymore; maybe *it* was just us. After that, my father never really talked about her at all. It was like she was dead.

He takes out a little ad in the back of the *Phoenix Gazette*:

WANTED!
USED CARS
ANY MAKE OR MODEL
WILL PAY CASH!

And he puts our phone number at the bottom.

The ad went in on a Sunday, in the late edition, and on Monday morning I'm all set to walk out the door with John when Dad stops me.

'Hey, Champ,' he says. 'No school for you today. Come on back in.'

John and I stare at Dad. John's mouth is hanging open so wide I can see his fillings, but mine is not. I have a feeling I know what is coming. John says, 'Da-a-ad . . .' the way he used to when he was little.

Dad glares at him. 'You just stop that. Someone's got to stay here and answer the phone. I'll bet it rings off the hook.'

'Why not me?' John throws his bag on the floor like nothing could make him pick it up again.

'Because I say. Because Greg is older. God knows what you'd say to those people. Now pick that up and get out of the house.'

John mooches, kicks at his bag, twists his hands. Dad sighs. 'It's no use,' he says. 'You're going to school. Come on, I'll give you a lift.' John brightens, picks up his bag, and my Dad puts his arm around his shoulder. 'I'd better stop off at the school anyhow,' he says, 'and tell them how sick you are. Scarlet fever, right?' He winks at me. I'm still not sure what's going on.

'Scarlet fever, Dad,' I say.

When they've gone I sit down by the phone. I don't know what to do with myself. It's not like I haven't bummed off school before, but this is different. I try to think what I'd do if I was just bumming off, no strings attached, and I think I'd

probably walk out toward the sandy lots at the end of town –
but then, I wouldn't be going there alone, there'd be a bunch of
us and we'd do something. And anyway, I can't leave the house,
I have to stay by the phone. I start to think, but what if one of
my teachers calls? What if Mr Olsen decides he's got a used car
to sell in his coffee break, and calls here? Should I answer the
phone like I'm sick? Should I pretend to be someone else?
This is what I'm trying to decide when the phone rings.

'Hello,' I say. It comes out squeaky, like sick and not-me
both at the same time. It isn't a good effect.

' . . . Hello? Is this 555–6759? Used cars?'

'Yes,' I say. 'Yeah, that's us.'

'I got a Pontiac. '75. Want to get rid of it. Any offers?'

I have no idea. Dad said cash. I wonder what cash he meant.

'Look,' I say. 'It's not me that wants the car. It's my dad. Steve
Snow. Can he call you when he gets home from work? That's
about six o'clock.'

The man at the other end of the phone breathes out heavily,
hissing loudly in my ear. 'Yeah, I guess so,' he says. 'Your old
man, huh? Opening a business?'

'Sort of.'

'Well, good luck to him, I say,' And the man laughs, not very
nicely. But I take his number, writing it down, along with
'Pontiac – 1975' at the top of a piece of looseleaf I pulled from
my school notebook. I take his name, too, Carl Felix. By the
end of the day I have a whole long list of numbers, cars, years
and names, which I hand to Dad when he gets home. He grins
like he's really happy.

'Terrific, kiddo,' he says. 'A good day's work. How about that.' And he keeps on grinning, looking down at the sheet of paper. John comes in and peers around him to see what I've written, then stares at me. I shrug. Dad folds the paper carefully and slips it in the back pocket of his jeans. 'Come on, buddies,' he says, 'let's go out for pizza.'

'Pizza!' John gallops upstairs, thump thump thump, to get his jacket. He'll do anything for pizza, and it's the only thing guaranteed to cheer him up when the Firebirds lose a game or some other tragedy blights his life. We ate a lot of pizza right after Mom left, and for the first couple of months even that barely did it for him. But now pizza is back to being just a great thing for John, and when my Dad takes us out, all three of us squeezed into the cab of the truck, it feels like a real boys' outing.

The funny thing is, these are the times I miss Mom most. Or not miss, exactly – I just wonder where she is and what she's doing, right at that very moment. We haven't heard anything from her, she could be in Alaska for all we know. So when Dad says we're going for pizza, I say it's great, and he gives me the keys so I can start up the truck, and then I hear John come running down the stairs, and the screen door slam. I'm glad that we fit so tight in the truck, because I feel pretty lonely and far away.

'Life,' my father says as we work our way through a huge mottled wheel of pizza, 'life is too mundane.'

'What's mundane?' asks John.

My father chews thoughtfully for a minute. 'Well,' he says. 'It's pretty much the same as boring. You get up. You go to work. You come home. You eat, several times a day. Then you go to bed and the whole things starts again the next day. And that's the problem. That's what's driving people crazy. Everybody does the same stuff, shops at the same stores, everybody goes to Disneyland to have the same fun. What about that guy who killed all those folks at McDonald's? What about Ted Bundy? What about Charles Manson? Those were people just bored out of their skulls, I'll bet. Boredom can do that to you.'

John gives me another look, or tries to, but I put my face in my drink and won't meet his eyes.

'There's no greatness around here,' my Dad goes on. 'Oh sure, there's the desert, and there's places like the Grand Canyon, but what do those do to people? Make them feel small. You stand at the edge of the Grand Canyon and think, well, just why *bother*, why bother with anything when there's this thing, millions and millions of years old and bigger than anything I'll ever be? People say it's uplifting, but I think it gets folks down.'

He takes a swig of his beer and a big bite of pizza which he chews hard, his jaws moving from side to side like a goat. John begins to fidget, kicking his legs under the table, and occasionally kicking me. He stares at Dad.

'You have to give people something to admire,' he says when he's swallowed. 'Look at all those things they have in Europe. Not just those stone circles but huge cathedrals and castles that people can look at and say *we* built those, *we're* okay – even if they're just building highways now the same as us.

'But what have we got? Look around you. Restaurants shaped like giant hotdogs, like cowboy hats, all made out of shitty, mangy-looking plaster. And people *admire this*. They do. People write books about them. You can buy them in any bookstore, big glossy full-colour photographs of enormous disintegrating sausages. Makes me sick.'

He sighs. I have to confess that at this point I'm staring too. I've never heard Dad talk this way. I've never heard anyone talk this way. It's like although I can hear all the words coming out, and I know what each one means, all together they're a foreign language.

I look at John. John has red hair like Mom, and the same pale skin which means you can see everything he's feeling right there in his face. Right now the skin is red and blotchy, and his eyes have gone pink like a rabbit's eyes. I really don't want him to cry. So I kick him hard on the shin.

'Hey – !' He is surprised enough that his skin gets a little paler and his eyes stop popping out. I am relieved. Then he turns to Dad, like he's just woken up. 'But so what, Dad?'

'So what? *So what?*' Dad shakes his head and looks at John. 'My son, the So-Whatters of this world are the ones you have to watch out for. The So-Whatters of this world are the ones who *build* the huge plaster hotdogs and take pictures of them and go to Disneyland on their vacations.'

We had never been to Disneyland. We wanted to go, but I thought that now was not the time to bring this up.

'Greatness. Greatness is what this world needs, what this country needs especially, and there just isn't enough of it to go around. And do you know why that is? It's because people don't understand that they have to make it themselves. I didn't understand that myself until – until a little while ago.' I wonder if he means *until your mother left*, but if he did he would never say it. 'So boys, we're not going to be So-Whatters anymore. Not this family. They're not going to watch us drive by and say, "Wouldn't you know, there go the So-Whatters who couldn't give a damn." Because we do. And we can make life better for everyone. Remember what I said? Energy? That's the ticket, boys, that's the trick.'

Dad picks up his beer glass and drains it in one long gulp, his Adam's apple jumping up and down like a float with a twitchy fish at one end. When it's empty, he bangs it down on the table so hard I think it will break, and everybody else in the pizza joint turns to look at us.

'What do you say, kids,' he says, and opens his arms wide. I notice the palms of his hands are cracked like they're not made out of skin but something harder. His eyes are nearly hidden by his smile. 'Who's for an ice-cream sundae?'

We both shout yes, and Dad does too, and we pile out towards the truck to go to Grey's. It's like he hasn't said anything. It's like it's OK.

Dad spends almost all of next Saturday on the phone. I can see he's got my piece of looseleaf in front of him, the one with all the names and cars and numbers on, and as he's talking he holds the phone against his shoulder with his cheek and scribbles down the side of the page. When he's finished, about four o'clock, he shouts out that he'll be back in a while, and walks out the front door. When he comes back he's got some cans of soup with him, and another loaf of bread and some ham. This is what we have for dinner, sitting around the table and not saying much. Suddenly, John looks up from his soup and says,

'How come we don't have cloth napkins anymore?'

We use paper towels now, which Dad folds carefully in two and places under our silverware. We used to have white napkins with lace edges that had E.B.F. embroidered on them, my grandmother's initials, Mom's mom.

'Too much trouble,' Dad says. 'You want to wash and iron them?' His voice is very even and logical.

'I guess not,' John says. He looks down at his plate.

'Where are the napkins, anyway?' I ask.

Dad looks out the window, towards the desert. 'I don't know,' he says at last.

I guess she took them with her.

We are standing, all three of us, staring across a little piece of the Colorado River at the big stone arches of London Bridge, in Lake Havasu City. Dad's arms are wide out, and in between his hands is the bridge, all the length of it: if I squint it really does look like he's holding it.

'This is it, boys,' he says. '*This* is the vision of a man who saw a lack of greatness around him. Game shows and beer are not what made this country, boys, not by a hell of a long shot. The Declaration of Independence. The Constitution. Four score and seven years. Manifest Destiny. I bet they don't even teach Manifest Destiny in the schools anymore.' He peers at us as if we might be keeping something from him, but he doesn't let us answer.

'Once upon a time, boys, this country had the energy and the imagination to *do* things. Devise. Invent. The automobile. The airplane. Made men who could do things. And I'll tell you, sometimes those men are still out there. Robert McCulloch, he was one of those men; a man who believed anything was possible. And so he brought this bridge all the way over from London. Asked the Queen for it. "Your Majesty," he said, "I'm afraid my people are in need of a little inspiration. A little of the loaves-and-fishes treatment. So if you don't mind I'll buy your bridge and I'll put it up in the desert and see what they make of that." And she sold it to him. And here we are.'

We stand in the morning sun, looking at the bridge.

'Come on,' says Dad. 'Let's take a walk.'

We had left the house a little after seven in the morning. Sunday. Until about 6:45, John and I hadn't known we were going anywhere. For a long time he wouldn't say where we were heading.

WELCOME TO LAKE HAVASU CITY
HOME OF LONDON BRIDGE

You can't believe there'll be a bridge when you see the sign. Lake Havasu is one of those towns at the edge of the desert that make you wonder why anyone put it there, or at least that's what it must have been like before the bridge arrived. Now it's big, with a lot of stores and ice-cream parlours, everything open even on a Sunday. They brought the river into town just so it could go under the bridge. When we drove into town we could see it, reflecting the sunlight like it was made out of metal. The whole effect is pretty impressive. There were a lot of cars driving over the bridge, beneath the long tails of multi-coloured banners, and lots of people underneath, walking around with kids and strollers and staring at the little fake river and pointing at the big bridge.

Now Dad walks in between John and me, with his hands in the pockets of his jeans. Usually he looks straight ahead, so that he won't see you coming from the side unless you shout, but today his head is all over the place, turning this way and that with his eyes darting back and forth. It makes him look like a big bird, like a vulture or something, the way his neck is stuck out with his head twisting on the end of it. His neck is like a vulture's too, pink and wrinkly at the back. We get all the way to the end of the bridge and stop. Dad leans over the rail and looks down, resting his heavy forearms on the metal, his hands loose over the water below like they don't belong to him. I can see John bunching his fists inside his pants. I have a feeling he's beginning to think there aren't any explanations to anything anymore.

'So,' Dad says at last.

'Yes?' I say. It sounds funny, but I think if I say 'So?' too, he'll think I'm being smart.

'You didn't say anything about the bridge.'

'Good bridge, Dad,' I say.

'Yeah, Dad.' John's eyes flicker between him and me.

'Well,' Dad says. And then his eyes pop up from the river, and drill straight into mine. 'You'll see,' he says. 'You'll see.'

It seems like every day I get home from school there is another car in the drive. Well, three actually fit in the drive: then they start to stack up, snaking out in a line down the block, across the street, double-parked. The neighbours come out on Saturdays and stand behind their lawnmowers, staring, the way neighbours do when there's something they don't like but they don't see what they can do about it. I don't think they'd mind if they were nice cars that my father is buying, but they aren't. They're shot through with rust and their seats are sprung; the tyre treads are worn bald. Dad is paying money for these things. And the more cars there are, the happier he is. He whistles all the time now, and slaps his hands on his thighs and rubs them together. In some ways, this is nothing new: I can recognize one of Dad's Projects a mile away. Usually they're pretty practical, or that's how they start out: building a garage, redesigning the kitchen – the refuse of these Projects litters the house and the garden outside. But nothing ever got finished; we were always tripping over the leavings of his work and once Mom got a really bad electric shock from some wires he'd left too near the sink. She screamed at him then, screamed and screamed. She'd never done that before.

So now I wonder about all this. I think a lot about the trip to Lake Havasu City, about Dad's long speeches, and tell myself he has a plan, which means at least he isn't crazy. John is not so sure. We begin to have the same conversation every night, when it's dark and safe and we can talk about things without having to see each other's faces.

'I'm telling you, he's crazy.' John's voice drifts up to me. We have bunk beds.

'No he isn't.'

There is silence. 'Maybe you're crazy too.'

'He's doing something. He's doing something important. He has a plan.'

'So what's he doing?'

'It's something to do with what he said. With energy. Like those things we saw on TV. Like the bridge we went to.'

'Those things were tombs.' John's voice is sulky now.

'Not all of them. And the bridge isn't. He's not crazy.'

'He wouldn't be doing this if Mom were around.'

I know that, so I don't say anything.

Dad is standing outside in the drive, handing seventy-five dollars to a very fat man who drove up in a green Honda that

211

looks like it's been run over by a truck. His very fat wife is standing next to him – she drove up in another car, a new one, the one I guess they'll drive off in. The phone rings.

'Hello?'

'Hi, Greg.'

'Mom.'

For a minute she doesn't say anything, but I know she's still there.

'How are you?'

'I'm OK.'

'John?'

'Him, too.'

I think I can hear her smiling. I am afraid she's making fun of me, calling from far away, a place that she knows but I don't.

'Where are you, Mom?'

'I'm –' I can hear cars going by in the background. She must be outside. 'I'm pretty far away.' Alaska, I think. But I know it could be anywhere. Down the street. Which would be worse. 'I miss you.'

'I miss you too, Mom.' If I were John, I would ask, *so why don't you come home?* and I try and think what she would say.

'How's your father?' she asks.

I can see him through the window, talking and laughing with the Fats. When the Fats laugh their legs and arms shake, and their cheeks are round moons. The woman has a beehive hairdo. Even her hair seems fat.

'He's fine.' For a second I think that if I tell her about all the cars parked outside she'd come home, but it seems unfair.

I like to think that all the rusting metal outside isn't her fault.

'Good.'

I suddenly realize how awful this conversation is, and I want it to end though I don't know how to hang up and part of me still wants her to be there, on the other end of the line. I wish she would stay there, not saying anything, and I would put the receiver down and go cook dinner and do my homework and go to sleep – I'd sleep on the sofa, by the phone – just knowing that she was there, so I could talk if I wanted, though I probably wouldn't. But she's standing there, in some Alaskan phonebooth, and she isn't going to stand there all night.

'I'd better go, Mom,' I say. 'I've got to get supper.' Dad is waving to the Fats, now: they're wobbling off towards their shiny new car. Dad shoves the bills down into his back pocket and turns back towards the house, smiling.

'All right, darling,' she says. Her voice is not sad, not happy.

'Should I say you called?' The screen door slams.

Then she sighs, and sounds afraid, and I wonder if she's sorry she called. 'You do – you do what you think is best, Gregory,' she says. I like it when she calls me Gregory. 'You know I trust you. I love you.'

'I love you too, Mom.' I'm not crying. I'm surprised. She hangs up.

Dad pokes his head around the door. 'Who was it?' he asks.

'Wrong number,' I say, and go into the kitchen.

*

Then Dad sells the truck. I come home from school and he's sitting at the kitchen table with this amazing pile of money in front of him. There are hundred-dollar bills. Benjamin Franklin is on the hundred-dollar bill: I never knew that before. Dad has a yellow pad in front of him, which he is writing on with a pencil. Every so often he stops and leafs through the money, which is in several not very neat piles arranged around the pad.

'Wow, Dad.'

Dad looks up, grins at me like we're sharing a secret. 'Yeah,' he says. 'Something, isn't it?' He picks up a bunch of notes, flicks through them like a gangster in a movie.

'Uh . . . where did it come from?' I wonder if this is a bad way to phrase the question. Dad doesn't seem to notice.

'Truck,' he says.

At first I don't get it. 'Truck?'

'Sold it,' he says. 'Sold the truck.' He is still grinning, like this is an obvious, wonderful thing to have done.

I know right away that this is part of the Plan. But there are a million questions I want to ask, starting with Why? and going on to How will we go shopping tomorrow? and How will we get to baseball games? I know that the answer isn't in all those wrecks because whatever is going on Dad doesn't intend to drive any of them.

'Hey, kiddo, don't worry,' Dad says. Sometimes it's like he knows what I'm thinking; but I guess it must have been pretty clear from my face. 'Just you wait,' he says.

★

214

The money from the truck goes to buy an empty lot at the edge of town. It's got a chain-link fence around it and it's covered with coarse, scrubby grass. And garbage – a layer of fading beer cans, plastic bags, old chairs – anything. People have just been tossing stuff over the fence for years. I don't know what Dad paid, but I know he thinks he's got a bargain.

He meets me after school one day. We all come out, and he's leaning against the fence, drinking a Coke. I go up to him with Billy and Mike, my two best friends.

'Hey Dad,' I say. Billy and Mike say hello to him, and they call him 'Mr Snow' even though he's always telling them to call him Steve.

'Hiya, kiddo,' he says to me. 'Hiya, boys. I was wondering if you boys wanted to give me a hand this afternoon,' he says. He rubs his hands together, like you see in cartoons. 'If you don't have too much homework.'

'What for?' Billy asks.

'I want to clear out my new lot. Get all the garbage up. I'll pay four dollars an hour to any garbage picker-upper who lends a willing hand.'

'Sure, Mr Snow!' Mike swings his bag up on to his back, ready to go like a boy scout. Mike has been my best friend for a long time now, and I've spent even more time with him lately because his Mom died when he was young and that makes me feel we have something in common. But right now I am annoyed at how eager he is, maybe because I want him to see that I am worried. But there's nothing I can say.

Billy and Mike say they'll go home first, and drop off their stuff. Dad tells them where the lot is, and we walk off in our separate directions. John has baseball practice; I can hear the balls popping against bats in the schoolyard. Dad and I walk home in silence.

We are already at the lot when Billy and Mike drive up with their dads. Billy's dad, Mr Melville, is an insurance salesman, and he looks like he spends a lot of time in his car, driving around with his elbow out the window. Mike's dad is a builder and smiles when he looks at Mr Melville. 'Hi, Steve,' he says to my dad. He comes to the store a lot to get wire and planks and things, and sometimes he and Dad have a beer.

'Hi there, Tom,' says Dad. His voice seems really loud. 'Hi there, Mr Melville.'

'Snow,' says Billy's dad, and the way he says it, it sounds like he's asking about the weather. 'You bought this place?' he asks.

'Yep,' says Dad, sounding pleased with himself. 'Come on, boys, I've got a whole pile of plastic bags, just take one and grab whatever you see.' Billy and Mike file in through the gate which Dad is holding open. 'Every last damned can and butt and chewing-gum wrapper. I want this place *pristine*,' he says. 'I want virgin ground.'

Mr Melville doesn't leave. Billy looks like he wishes he would. 'Pretty scrappy piece of land,' he says. 'Can't imagine it'll be good for much. You planting? Or what?'

Dad looks up at him, one eyebrow cocked up nearly into his hair. 'I guess you might say we're planting, Jack. Doing some planting, yes, of a kind.' I try to look like I know what he's talking about. Billy keeps picking up garbage, faster and faster.

'Okay, Snow,' Mr Melville says. 'You know best.' He scratches his neck. 'You don't catch me calling you a crank.'

Mr Melville gets back in his car and drives off in a cloud of dust and exhaust, and three of us wait for my dad to get mad. But he doesn't.

'A good thing too,' Dad says to us, and bends down again, tossing junk into the swelling plastic bag on the ground.

Dad begins to refer to all of this as Operation Dynamo and he quits his job at the store. He doesn't tell us this for a while. When I hear it, half of me feels afraid, like when he sold the truck, but then I remember that we've mananged without that, after all, and I realize that I still have a lot of faith in Dad. That night, we watch *Captains Courageous* on TV and Dad puts his arms around our shoulders.

The next morning the diggers arrive. They trundle by our house in a slow, dirty yellow parade, and Dad's voice booms out in the bright morning air. It's very early, and John and I are still in bed, but I lean down and shake his shoulder.

'. . . what?' John sleeps like he might have died. He never even messes up his covers at night.

'Come on, man.' I jump down, thumping hard by his head, and begin to pull on my clothes. 'Something's happening.'

Outside, Dad is shouting and waving, giving directions, a thick bunch of papers held tight in his pointing hand. I can't hear what he's saying; he's talking to the guy who's driving the digger at the head of the line. They are huge things, bright yellow paint gone dark with dust and globs of oil, the windows so smeared with grime it's hard to believe the men can see out of them. I come up next to Dad and he turns to me like he knew I was there all along.

'This is it, kiddo,' he says. 'T minus zero. Lift off. It's happening. We'll show them.'

'Are these all going to the lot?' I ask. I crane my neck because I'm trying to see the papers he has in his hand.

'Yessir,' he says. 'Yes indeedy!' He is excited like a little kid, like John is on his birthdays or at Christmas. But then suddenly he breathes in deeply, it's almost a sigh, and he turns to me.

'Greg,' he says. I can see the broken blood-vessel in his eye, from when I accidentally hit him with a baseball five years ago. 'Let's go in the house. I want to show you something.'

We go back in and sit down at the kitchen table, and Dad spreads the papers he was holding out in front of him. Maps and plans, xeroxed out of books, pages of yellowy newsprint with Dad's own plans in pencil. There are photographs too, very grainy but clear, of big stones standing up on grass, the spaces between them like giant doors leading to nothing. When I look at Dad's face I can see that there's practically a light coming out of his eyes.

'Greg,' he says again. 'We're going to call up forces. That's the way I see it.'

'What – forces, Dad?'

'The forces of the universe. This is where it's at. I tell you, I've been reading a lot – yes, that's right, me, sitting down every day at the library and reading like crazy. It's great, you should try it sometime.' Then he winks, socks me on the shoulder, looks more like his old self. 'Don't you worry, Champ, I know you're no dope. But I tell you, the thing I've found out from reading is this: the more of it you do, the less you really know. Every Mister and Doctor and his kid brother has a different opinion, a different solution to your problem, and maybe nobody even knows what the problem is in the first place. Everyone has a different theory for everything. Two guys look through a microscope, they see two different things in the same bug. Read history books – you find out nobody knows what *really* happened. Now look at Stonehenge. Some people say it's to worship the sun. There's other folks say it's to worship the moon, or it's a calendar, or a device to predict eclipses. Just about the only thing that all these professors agree on is that the stones – the huge ones –' and he jabs at a photocopy with a fat finger, 'come from real far away. Two hundred miles away. And the guys who built this thing didn't even know about *the wheel*. Look at that,' and he pokes the paper again, 'forty-five tons. Each. If that's not energy, if that's not get up and go, I don't know what is.'

He pushes himself away from the table and it rocks on its one wobbly leg. 'Go wake up your brother,' he says. 'I've got to make a phonecall. There's things I want to tell the both of you.'

I go into the bedroom. John is awake, sitting up in bed. His eyes are wary. 'What's going on?'

For a minute I don't know what to say, because I suddenly realize I don't know whose side I'm on. John wants things to be normal, like nothing is happening; and for a while I'd wanted that too. But things are changing. I'm not so scared anymore.

'Something big, John,' I said. 'Something really big. Just you wait and see. Come on.'

I laugh, really loud, so I sound like Dad, pull him out of bed and he lands with a bump on the floor.

'What I want to know,' Dad says, 'is when they *forgot*.' The three of us are walking fast towards Operation Dynamo, fast enough so that John and I sometimes have to trot to keep up. I can see the diggers moving at the end of the street.

'You build this tremendous thing, this great construction out of stones you had to go and get in the middle of winter – imagine that, boys, dragging those things with ropes over icy ground, with only a wolf-skin or something to keep out the cold – you had to convince people that this was an important enough thing to maybe risk your life for. So it had to be something they all believed in, right? And this wasn't done all at once. This went on for *thousands of years*. It was developed, it was improved; it was a big part of people's lives. It's hard for us to even imagine something like that, isn't it?'

It is. I try, and I really can't. I try and think of some cultural thing that's always been there and that's very important to me, but all I can think of is the Superbowl or the Major Leagues and I know it's not the same. Dad waves to the man in the biggest digger. The man gives him a kind of salute. Although it's early, a small crowd is gathering around the chain-link fence.

'Hi, folks,' Dad calls out as we get close. 'Lovely morning for working, ain't it?'

There is a little ripple of laughter. All these people have the same face as John: cautious, uncertain, frightened. It occurs to me that people don't like big things in their lives, and whatever else he may be, Dad sure is a big thing.

'Stay there a minute, boys, will you?' He plants us just inside the perimeter of the fence and jogs up to the digger. Over the noise, I can just hear him call the man Howard, but I can't hear much else, though I see him gesturing, and pointing at the plans. Dad slaps him on the back through the slid-open door, then jumps down off the cab and comes back to us.

'Now jump forward in time a little,' he says to us, taking up where he left off. 'And think of – well, think of a father and his two sons taking a walk around Salisbury Plain, in England, and coming up to this big thing. They walk around it, they go inside, it's a nice Sunday morning just like this one. And one of the sons turns to his Dad and says, "Dad? What is this big thing?" And all Dad can do is scratch his head and say, "You know something, son? *I just don't know.*"'

John looks up at Dad, looks over the diggers, looks back at Dad. All the time Dad's been talking he's been glancing at the crumpling papers Dad still has clutched in his hand. He takes a deep breath. 'But what's that got to do with all this?' he asks. There is a desperate edge to his voice; this is the question he's been wanting to ask for so long, and maybe it was me who made him feel that he couldn't.

'It's a powerful place,' Dad says. He's talking like he hasn't heard John, but John is looking up at him eagerly, waiting for answers. 'I've never been there, and I'd sure like to go. But I know one thing: that power like that is important, and pretty hard to find these days. There's a little of it in McCulloch's bridge, and maybe some in the Empire State Building or the Statue of Liberty. But I think we need some right here. And that,' he says, 'is exactly what we're going to get. And this time we'll make sure no one forgets. That's your job, kid.' And then he looks right at John, and it's almost like a spark flies off him and lands on my brother, like it landed on me. Dad is electric.

John is smiling, the first real grin I've seen on his face for a while. 'Wow, Dad,' he says.

'You bet your life Wow,' Dad says as he puts his arms around us. 'A Wow and a half.'

I can hear the crowd getting bigger, chattering and whispering behind us, as the diggers with their ferocious clanking heads begin to bite into the earth, throwing up clouds of dust that make the bright day hazy and blurred.

The digging takes a couple of days. Dad is running around all over the place, pointing and shouting and giving directions, measuring the big square holes that now pocket the ground with a bright yellow tape measure he keeps clipped to his old leather belt. In the afternoon of that first Sunday, Billy and Mike turn up, with their whole families, and so do a lot of other kids from school, and crowds of people we don't even know. News spreads fast in a place like this, and Dad is giving a great show. He's a cross between a construction-site foreman and a talk-show emcee. Even Billy's dad is impressed. At one point he hands me a twenty and tells me to run to the 7-11 and bring back bottles of soda and plastic cups for everyone, and bags of pretzels too. When I go in, Zack Kowalski, who runs the place, is so eager to hear what's going on that he even gives me a lift in his car back to the field, turning his sign to 'Closed' and locking the door.

And the *Republic* sends a reporter. She comes on Monday morning (John and I don't even think of going to school, and we know that Dad isn't going to make us), a girl with a pony-tail and a baseball cap who doesn't look that much older than me. She has a pencil tucked behind one ear, a lined notepad, and also one of those itty-bitty tape recorders in the top pocket of her shirt. The ear with the pencil has a gold hoop in it, right up near the top. She doesn't have any trouble finding Dad; when she arrives he's right in the middle of things, directing traffic and grinning.

'Mr Snow! Mr Snow!' She waves the pad at him. Her voice is straining above the rumbling of the diggers. 'I'm Lauren Armstrong, from the *Republic*! Can we talk a minute?'

Dad looks over at her, looks her up and down, and she wiggles her notepad at him. He walks over to her, his gait rolling and slow, his thumbs hooked into his pockets. I am standing by the chain-link, watching all this out of the corner of my eye. John is riding in a digger, hanging on to the controls with the driver's hands around his own. He's having a great time, and I'm glad.

'They didn't make reporters like you in my day,' Dad says. He puts out his hand for her to shake, which she does, but I think she's also blushing. I look away. Dad is starting to give her his lecture about the first man who forgot, about power, almost the same stuff he said to us, so I don't have to listen.

For the first time in a while I think about Mom the way I did when she first left, a way that almost isn't like thinking at all because it doesn't seem to happen in my head; it happens in my stomach and chest and the fronts of my thighs. It makes me want to draw all these parts together and curl up on the ground, I miss her so much. I feel awful and I wonder if this is how John feels all the time and I hope that it isn't. I turn around and put my face against the warm chain-link so I can face out towards where the desert is.

This is how I am when Lauren Armstrong comes up to me.

'Hi,' she says. 'Greg? Greg Snow?'

I turn around because I don't know if Dad is watching me or not, and if I don't turn, and Dad sees, he'll yell at me for being rude. 'That's me.'

'No school, huh?' And she winks at me. I don't know what to say.

'I think some things are more important than school. I think this is. Your dad says you've been real helpful.'

'He did? I don't know. I took some phone calls and stuff.' I want Lauren Armstrong to leave me alone.

'Does your Mom – I mean, is she –' Lauren Armstrong, Cub Reporter, knows she's stepped into some kind of puddle. She is embarrassed and trying not to be.

'Mom left a while ago. It's just the three of us now. There's my brother John, see? On the digger.' I point.

Lauren Armstrong is quiet for a minute, like she is putting all the things she knows on file cards in her head and then laying them out and arranging them: Dad, Operation Dynamo, me and John, Mom-who-left-a-while-ago. Then she says, very brisk and cheerful, 'This is really something, you know. Big news for the paper. They're sending a photographer. And you know what? I think with pictures, this may just go national.'

She's looking off at the diggers as she says this, and smiling a little, and I have a feeling she thinks this may be her big break. Maybe it will be. But right now I'm not really interested in Lauren Armstrong, and I don't listen too hard to what she says.

'Well listen, Greg,' she says. 'Thanks. It's been great. Exciting. I hope it all goes well. I might see you later. OK? Good luck with everything.' She puts out her hand and I shake it and say it's OK, no problem, anytime. She has a nice smile. She's pretty, in fact. And I think she means what she says about it being exciting out here, because it *is*, and I start to remember what I felt when Dad showed me his plans this morning. Lauren Armstrong doesn't think my dad is crazy, and I start to like her just for that. I've never felt so many things all at once before in my life, and I decide that this is what Operation Dynamo is all about: that this is the power Dad is talking about, being released into the dusty air and infecting all of us, the men in the diggers, John, Lauren Armstrong.

Who's walking away now, taking off her baseball cap and running a hand through her hair. It's starting to heat up. Once she's outside the lot, she turns and waves, to my dad or to me I can't tell, but I wave back anyhow.

The cars come in a parade on Wednesday morning. Some of them can't be driven and so they have to be towed, but the tow trucks follow the line of exhausted, wheezing automobiles that limps through the centre of town towards Dad's lot, now pitted with craters and marked with little flags, the gap in the chain-link widened to admit cranes and winches and even a cement truck, its barrel–body rolling and rumbling like distant thunder. People come out of their houses and stores to see them go by, and Dad has had no trouble at all recruiting all the drivers he needs. And he lets me drive the one in front, the first car we bought – the beat-up Pontiac – because he knows we're going to go real slow and I'll never have to take it out of second gear. People are clapping and waving, and when we pass the 7-11 Zack Kowalski comes running out with his arms full of bags of potato chips and boxes of Ring Dings, and he throws them in the back seat through the open window along with a load of those two-quart bottles of Coke and Sprite. He bangs the hood of the car and shouts, 'Good Luck!' and I can hear somebody yell out, 'Go for it, Snow, you crazy bastard!' and I can tell they mean it in a nice way, though that's a funny thing to say.

When we get there I pull the Pontiac into the lot and Dad gets out. He guides the next three cars in line inside the fence, and then he stops the rest with his palms flat like a traffic warden's, shouting, 'OK, OK, hold it right there fellas, that'll do fine for now. Just climb out and leave the keys in 'em. Pete –' he turns to Pete Charlap, our next-door neighbour, who was pretty nasty about the whole thing at first (he used to leave mean little notes under the wipers of all the old cars and sign them 'Anonymous' although we all knew perfectly well it was him), but who's come around like anything in the last week or so – he turns to Mr Charlap and says, 'Pete, if you don't mind, would you just run on down to the tow trucks and tell 'em to bring those babies up here by the front? Then we can hook 'em right up to the winches.'

'Sure thing, Steve,' Mr Charlap says, and jogs off, the creases in his slacks jumping up and down as he goes. He runs Zappers, the small appliance store, which is shut today like a lot of other things.

It's an amazing thing to watch. The cranes and winches start up their engines, and wait while Dad gets back into the Pontiac and drives it carefully into the centre of the circle, craning his neck out the window to make sure he avoids the deep pits that have been dug all around. He parks it carefully – after all this, parking a car is just the same – and then gets out and, raising his hand high with a kind of flourish, drops the keys into one of the big pits at the centre of the lot. 'OK, fellas,' he calls. 'Action! Let's get us some cement!'

And so the cement truck trundles over slowly, carefully, until it can't get any closer. Then the guy driving and his partner climb out and extend the big funnel at the back of the truck so the lip is over the hole. All Dad has to do is turn a lever when they nod to him and a slow flood of cement comes belching out of the belly of the truck and begins to slop into the ground.

John comes up behind me. He was riding in one of the tow trucks. For a guy who likes to ride in things (speedboats, tractors, he doesn't care), he's had a good few days. 'Let's go see,' he says, and we walk into the compound and stand at the edge of the hole across from Dad. The rattling cement truck makes the air around it throb.

Dad throws the lever back up when the hole is about a third full.

'Right,' Dad shouts, so loud we both jump. 'First car! Winch her up!'

The car has been hooked on to the winch by its back fender, which pulls away from the car a little as the cord begins to tighten. Dad and I had a big discussion the night before about whether the cars should go in nose down or nose up. He couldn't make up his mind.

'I think it's important for the flow of energy,' he'd said. 'We'd better get it right.'

'But if the cars aren't running, they don't have any energy in themselves, do they? So can't you just flip a coin or something?'

Dad had looked worried. 'I don't know,' he said. 'I'm just not sure.'

John looked up from his meatloaf. 'What about the exhausts, Dad?' he said. 'Those are at the back of the car, and so is the gas tank. If you had the exhausts sticking up in the air, it would be like the energy from the car shooting up into the sky.'

Dad nodded slowly. He knew John was scared of Operation

Dynamo, but he never was one for comforting people. He didn't believe, like Mom did, that everything would be all right. He thought you had to make it all right. I guess he thought that John would come round in the end; and he had.

'Good thinking, kiddo,' he said. 'That's a very good thought. I'll bear that one in mind. Yes, that just might do nicely.' And so all the cars were to go in nose down.

The winches lift them up in the air where they dangle, shining in the sun and swaying gently from side to side. When the nose of the first car hits the cement in the hole, it makes a squelching sound, like feet in wet rubber boots, and the steel rope starts to slacken as the car sinks into the wet cement. The back half of the car sticks straight up out of the ground.

Everyone leaning against the fence cheers when they see the car sink in solid, and Dad looks happier than I've ever seen him. 'One down,' he shouts, 'Twenty-four to go!' And they cheer again. It's like a big party. When school gets out, all the kids – the ones who hadn't been out with us all morning anyway – come out, and Dad lets them drop pennies into the wet cement and the winch drivers let the littler ones sit on their laps. Nobody seems to mind that they're going to have this strange construction at the bottom of town: and by the end of the day it's looking pretty weird because the cars which will be the 'lintels' have been hauled up on top of the others, with Dad underneath welding them on to the nose-downers in showers of sparks that look just like fireworks in the dusk.

It is at this point that I finally come to see what Dad means about energy. You can practically smell it in the air, blowing around like smoke. It's hard to tell where it comes from; part of me thinks it comes from Dad, or from all the happy people, but part of me likes to think it really is pouring out of the rusted and bent exhaust pipes which poke out of the ground like cosmic chimneys.

And that's how Operation Dynamo happened. It's still there, and has become a kind of local tourist attraction, though people don't exactly go out of their way to see it. But if they're passing through, they will. And Dad goes down a few evenings a week, after work – he didn't have any trouble getting his job back – and he'll sit inside, leaning on the Pontiac, and smoke a cigar. I know he does this because I followed him once; but I think he likes to be alone there.

He's put up a sign, carefully stencilled on white board, hooked to the chain-link fencing, which says OPERATION DYNAMO at the top and then all our three names beneath that in smaller letters. Below that there's a diagram of the place, like a horseshoe set inside a circle, with a painted compass showing you where North is. North is out towards the desert.

That's it. I was surprised, because I thought the whole point of the sign would be to tell people why we built it, so they wouldn't forget, like Dad said. But he said that the thing that he learned in building Operation Dynamo, the secret, was that the reason for it was inbuilt – like a car with an automatic choke, he said. All you had to do was look. And if you looked hard enough, he said, you'd find your own reasons too, not just his – and that was why people still went to Stonehenge, and why people walked over London Bridge and were happy without ever knowing who Robert McCulloch was. In the end, you can't ever know how anything started: real immortality, he said, is when things change and stay the same all at the same time. That's the biggest energy of all.

Still, I like to make sure the sign stays clean and that the paint doesn't chip. If Mom comes back, I don't want her to have any trouble reading our names.

*For further information about Granta Books
and a full list of titles, please write to us at*

Granta Books

2/3 HANOVER YARD

NOEL ROAD

LONDON

N1 8BE

enclosing a stamped, addressed envelope

———————————

You can visit our website at

http://www.granta.com